THE ENGLISH PROPOSAL

WINDOW TO THE HEART SAGA

JENNA BRANDT

CONTENTS

DESCRIPTION

Window to the Heart Saga: a recountal of the epic journey of Lady Margaret, a young English noblewoman, who through many trials, obstacles, and tragedies, discovers her own inner strength, the sustaining force of faith in God, and the power of family and friends. In this three-part series, experience new places and cultures as the heroine travels from England to France and completes her adventures in America. The series has compelling themes of love, loss, faith and hope with a exceptionally gratifying conclusion.

The English Proposal (*Book 1*). Sheltered on her family's country estate, Lady Margaret, the daughter of an English Earl, is betrothed due to a family promise. Although Henry, the Viscount Rolantry, has been her best friend since childhood and she is expected to marry him, she never felt butterflies until she meets the Duke of Witherton. Against her father's wishes, Margaret finds herself captivated by the forbidden duke. Caught between family loyalty and her own wishes, Margaret searches for a way to satisfy both her responsibilities and her longings. When tragedy strikes, Margaret finds herself seeking answers at church. But when she finally makes her choice, through her newfound faith, will she be able to live with the repercussions of her decision?

Profoundly romantic and superbly riveting, **The English Proposal** explores the conflict between fulfilling duties and satiating desires.

Window to the Heart Saga

Book 1: The English Proposal
Book 2: The French Encounter
Book 3: The American Conquest

For more information about Jenna Brandt, visit her on any of her websites.

www.JennaBrandt.com
www.facebook.com/JennaBrandtAuthor
www.twitter.com/JennaDBrandt
www.amazon.com/author/jennabrandt
Signup for Jenna Brandt's Newsletter

To my mother, Connie.
You have inspired, encouraged, and believed in me
all my life. You have always been my muse.

PROLOGUE

1853 Brighton, England

It was a warm spring day as four children played tag in the English garden of the Viscount Rolantry's country estate. Two of them looked identical with their black curly hair, deep violet eyes, and pale white skin, except one was a boy and one was a girl. The third child was a fair-haired boy with remarkable brown eyes and slender build. The fourth boy, with black hair and matching dark eyes, was not from England but was visiting while his French father conducted business.

"I caught you, Mags," the dark-haired boy, Randall, yelled at his twin sister, using the nickname he had given her.

Sulking, the petite Margaret complained, "Randall, you promised you would try to catch Henry first."

Margaret tried to pull free from her "captor" but was

unable to break loose and screamed, "Help me, help me," knowing that one of the other boys would come to her rescue. For even at that age of eight, men fell at Margaret's feet.

"I demand you release the lady at once," yelled the French boy, Pierre.

"I will save you, my love," the fair-haired Henry cried out as he rushed up and stood between the twins, wooden sword in hand. "On guard, you scallywag. Unhand the princess at once," Henry taunted.

"You cannot have her. She is mine forever," returned Randall, as he pulled his own wooden sword free from his waistband and swung it at the other boy.

For several moments, the three boys play-fought around Margaret with their wooden swords until Henry grabbed Margaret's arm with his free hand and said, "You are wrong. She will be mine! I am going to marry her one day."

Everyone froze for a moment as all the boys, with the exception of her brother, were smitten with Margaret, but none of them ever discussed it.

The twins looked at each other with wide eyes, and then laughingly, they said in unison, "Ewwww!"

Both nodded, not needing to talk of their plan, then bolted in opposite directions.

Heartbroken, Henry hung his head and walked over to the tree nearby. He leaned against it in discouragement.

Margaret turned to see if any of the boys were chasing her and realized Henry was upset. She went to stand next to him and gently put her hand on his arm, asking, "What is wrong, Henry? We were just playing."

He looked up to meet her eyes and said with sadness, "You are never going to love me like I love you, are you, Margaret?"

"Do not be silly, Henry. You will always be my best friend."

He looked at Margaret and knew that would never be enough.

CHAPTER 1

1861 Brighton, England

*L*ady Margaret Wellesley, daughter of the Earl of Renwick, sucked in her breath anxiously. What was she thinking? She would never be able to measure up to the kind of wife Henry expected. And well, she knew it. It was part of the reason that Margaret had never let herself truly get close to him. She kept hidden so many parts of herself because she was afraid to really let him know her. Deep down, she worried she would disappoint him if he saw her imperfections.

She arched an eyebrow as she looked at herself critically in the mirror. She tucked and pulled at the folds of her ivory, satin gown to make sure every detail was in place. Her dress had a corseted waist with a full, bell-shaped skirt that tiered down in cascading layers. The corset was accented with tiny rows of shimmering pearls that crisscrossed and complemented her petite frame. The gown was beautiful and she had waited for weeks for it to finally be finished. She had been promised that her dress would be the most spectacular and stunning one at her ball. Coupled with her contrasting raven locks that were accented with strands of pearls woven through and a matching set that lay around her neck and on her ears, she was pleased with her ensemble.

Margaret made her way from her dressing chamber towards the ballroom. She descended the grand staircase, pausing at the middle flat and resting her gloved hands on the banister. This was her big moment. Tonight, she would finally be presented to society.

Alfred, the family butler, came from around the corner and announced, "Presenting Lady Margaret, the daughter of the Earl of Renwick."

All the eyes of the assembled guests fastened on the freshly blossoming sixteen-year-old girl. Everyone in the English nobility, or "the ton" as they were more commonly referred to, had heard the rumors of Lady Margaret's alluring beauty.

From the moment her name and description circulated amongst them, the eligible noblemen had started to seek out her father to try to pursue her. She had inherited her late mother's aristocratic face and delicate bone structure and her father's Irish white skin and dark violet eyes.

Margaret smiled with graceful ease as she overtly scanned the room for Henry.

"He is not here yet."

The hair on the back of her neck stood up. Whose voice was that? She had never heard it before. It was deep and resonating.

Slowly, she turned to her left and looked up. Her eyes met the most piercing set of blue eyes she had ever seen. After a second's pause, she took in the rest of the man who matched the voice.

He was... beautiful. There was no other way to describe the stranger standing before her. He had curly brown hair that enhanced the blueness of his eyes. His face and body were flawless, built perfectly and gleamed golden like ripe olives. And he was so tall; he towered over her.

Dashing in his formal attire, Margaret stared at the striking stranger, wondering who was he. She had never seen him before, and she knew everyone who socialized in her circle.

"To whom are you referring, my lord?" she asked with pretend naiveté.

"Why, to your betrothed, certainly... or have you forgotten him already? Not that I mind, considering that it puts *my* task much more in the realm of attainability."

She liked this stranger and his easy banter. Deciding to shuck her coyness and participate in his game, she replied with purposeful playfulness, "I have not forgotten because I have not the intent or a good enough reason to do so."

"That is because you have not met me until now. I am going to change everything."

Margaret was rather astonished by the stranger's blatant statement but did not want him to realize it. She opted to counter in an effortless tone, "Why, sir, you presume I plan to get to know you."

He smiled with a hint of slight cockiness and held out his arm to her. "It seems that you are without escort this eve. Let me be of assistance. I would be honored if you would allow me to accompany you to dinner."

Laughing with gaiety, she put her hand in the crook of his arm and said, "Thank you, good sir, I would be—"

But she was broken off midsentence by a voice from behind that she recognized all too well. "*That* will not be necessary. I have arrived, and I will be escorting Lady Margaret."

She stiffened automatically out of reflex, not liking Henry finding her here like this. It could appear improper, and in their circle of acquaintances, appearances meant everything.

Turning around expeditiously, she put on her most endearing smile. "Good evening, my lord. I am glad that you have arrived."

"Yes, by all means, the lady was waiting for you *so anxiously* upon these stairs," the gentleman stated with a hint of sarcasm.

Henry stepped forward and gently but firmly took Margaret's hand, putting it on his own arm. Margaret looked up at her betrothed and saw the man she had known since she was a little girl. He was tall and of a slender build but had an elegant grace that surrounded him. He had straight blond hair that was slicked back tonight for the ball, matched with strong brown eyes and a warm smile. Most women would consider him to be very appealing, and some had even said so when they thought Margaret was not listening.

The two men stood toe-to-toe in their regal dress suits, and moments ticked by as Henry stared at the man across from him. Finally, Henry stated coldly, "Lady Margaret, may I introduce to you the Duke of Witherton."

Without realizing it, she took in a deep breath and held it tightly. She had heard about the duke. His name was Richard Charles Townsend III, Duke of Witherton, and he and Henry were bitter enemies stemming from their time in the military. Richard was older by a few years and had a greater title, and by all rights assumed he deserved to be commissioned first, but Henry received the position and rank that Richard had sought. Henry and the duke ended up in one fight after another until finally they decided to end what little contact they had altogether.

What was he doing here? She had to know. Of course, her father had invited him. The entire ton had been invited. But the duke never went anywhere, least of all to parties of those whose titles were of a lesser nature.

"Your Grace, you do us a great honor by being here. Although, I must say, I am surprised to find you here considering that you have never attended one of *our* gatherings before," she said pointedly.

"My lady, you are correct, and it has been to my disadvantage, so it seems," he said while looking at her meaning-fully. She blushed, receiving his message all too clear.

Trying to sound convincing but failing, Margaret replied, "You exaggerate, sir. We have nothing in the country worthy of your time."

Margaret leaned into Henry's support and kept her eyes averted, trying to hide the fact that she was blushing.

"On the contrary, I had been told that there was something here that would fit my, shall we say, tastes. And I see that I was well informed. I see something that I fancy and is *quite* worth my time."

And with that, before either Margaret or Henry could react, Richard took Margaret's free hand gently and bent over to kiss the top of it.

Then the most unexpected thing happened: Margaret felt this fluttering feeling in her stomach, almost like…. No, she was imagining it because she had worked herself up so much for tonight. She could not have felt butterflies! It was impossible, and especially not by a kiss from this man she was supposed to hate!

Quickly, she pulled her hand away while giving him a disdainful look, and he slowly straightened. The duke slightly raised his eyebrows and smiled in part amusement and part understanding that he made her feel something she did not expect.

"I hope to enjoy the rest of the evening, and I am sure I will, since you will be in attendance. I look forward to speaking with you again at a future time, my lady."

Then, almost as an afterthought, he turned to Henry and stated with a slight decline of his head, "Rolantry."

With that, the duke turned and slowly strolled down the stairs and into the dining hall, leaving them quite alone.

The discomfort was substantial between Margaret and Henry. She did not know what to say or how to break the silence. Instead, she opted for the easiest way out and stood quietly.

"It is not like you to be so silent, *my sweet*. What is on your pretty little mind?"

Oh no. She could hear it in his tone and affectionate address that he was indeed angry. He was clipping his words, and he never used terms of endearment in public because he knew it embarrassed her. It was a sure sign that fury seethed underneath his cool exterior.

He waited a few moments and asked again, "*My love*, whatever are you thinking about?"

"I was just thinking that if we do not hurry, we will be late to dine."

"That can wait. This, on the other hand, needs to be handled straightaway."

It seemed there was no way around it. She was going to have to deal with what had just happened. He was not going to let it pass without comment.

"The duke approached me. I was standing here searching for you when he startled me from behind."

"Yes, that may be what you want me to believe, but you

did not seem startled when I came upon the two of you together."

That did it; she was tired of his endless jealousy. He was always overreacting anytime any man outside her family paid any attention to her. She was going to put a stop to it once and for all. "My lord, please stop being so overprotective and possessive. The duke was only being courteous and giving his greetings to his hostess. I did not, nor did anyone else, read anything more into it, *except you!*"

"Is that so? Why, I was certain that the fact that we are betrothed gives me some right to care about who you are with and what you are doing!"

Oh, how it infuriated her that he thought he could control her. Margaret knew how marriages worked in their society, but she hated the fact that she would be entering into a marriage that made her little more than a possession. "You do not own me, my lord, at least not yet."

A look of deep hurt crossed Henry's face as he retorted, "My intent was never to own you, only to love and protect you. Is that so wrong?"

Margaret regretted what she said as soon as he explained his actions. She felt like such an insensitive and mean-spirited person. Henry was her oldest friend and she cared deeply for him. She did not want to hurt him.

Chagrined over her behavior, Margaret said, "No, that is not wrong if that was all you intended."

"The truth of the matter is that the duke has no scruples

and even less morals and would stop at nothing to get at me, including using you."

"I hardly think that I could be a valuable pawn in any scheme directed at you. You have always been self-sufficient, and I, in all reality, am of little consequence."

He turned to face her and looked deeply into her eyes. It was all she could do to not turn away from his searching gaze. "You must have no idea how important you truly are to me."

She allowed his confession to sink in momentarily, but just as quickly pushed it away as if he never said it.

Margaret knew that she was trapped in her betrothal to Henry due to a couple of key reasons. First and foremost was his dead father's influence over her father. They had been the closest of friends from childhood and raised their families together, agreeing to marry their children to each other. All Henry had to do was mention his father's name and the earl got teary-eyed. Secondly, her father was a man of his word and he had given it to Henry. It did not matter how many suitors pursued her; nothing would change her father's mind on the subject.

Really, her father should have found someone with a greater title for her once he inherited his earldom, but he chose to stay true to his promise instead. It also helped that no one could match Henry's wealth. His family had the gift of knowing a good investment when it came along, and Henry had banked on it more than once. He was considered one of the better catches in their social circle because his wealth made up for what he lacked in title.

Henry broke the uncomfortable silence. "You are right about supper. We are on the verge of being late. We should make our way to the dining hall," he said as he guided her forward with steely resolve.

CHAPTER 2

*T*he meal had passed by dreadfully slow. Margaret had listened to polite conversation and made the appropriate responses throughout, but her mind unwillingly kept returning to thoughts of the duke. She knew she had no right to be thinking about another man while she was engaged to Henry, but she had never felt anything like what she felt when the duke kissed her hand. It made her wonder what it would be like if he kissed her somewhere else....

Her father giving a toast interrupted Margaret's thoughts. The elderly gentleman stood to his feet and all eyes were on the graying, thin man with violet eyes and a friendly smile. "I would like to make a toast to my daughter. She has given me sixteen marvelous years with a lifetime full of memories. You are the finest daughter a man could have."

Glasses were raised and everyone replied "To Margaret!" before sipping from their goblets.

"I would also like to make a toast to the Lady Margaret, my betrothed. You are my best friend and my one true love. I look forward to sharing my life and home with you."

The glasses rose again and "Hear, hears" echoed.

Margaret smiled appreciatively at Henry and gently smoothed the edge of her dress as she prepared herself for the dancing part of the evening. But before anyone could stand and move towards the ballroom, one additional, unexpected person stood to make a toast to Margaret.

Her eyes grew wide with surprise as she watched the Duke of Witherton rise from his seat and say, "Since we are making toasts to the fair Lady Margaret, I too would like to make one. Here is to one of the most exquisite ladies that I have ever had the pleasure of meeting. You bring light and radiance with you wherever you go, and I find myself utterly enchanted with how you do it. You are truly as majestic as the rumors have said."

Several guests looked back and forth between Henry, Margaret, and the duke while moments ticked by in awkward silence. Finally, the glasses rose a final time in honor of Margaret. The discomfort in the room was thick. It was unusual for someone of the duke's stature to single out someone of Lady Margaret's status, and even more bizarre that he did it while she was betrothed and in front of her intended.

In those moments directly following Richard's toast, she felt more embarrassment than she had in a long time. But the most irrational part of it was that she secretly had to admit that it flattered her a great deal that Richard had made his toast in the first place. The entire situation made her blush from the fact that he would make his interest known so openly.

The earl rose to his feet again. "I would like to thank both the Viscount Rolantry and the Duke of Witherton for making their toasts in honor of my daughter. I would now like to invite everyone to join my family in the ballroom so the dancing may commence."

She could always count on her father to make an uncomfortable situation more bearable. She smiled at him with a look of relief that only he could register. He smiled back and came around, taking her by the arm.

"I feel it is my duty to escort you to the dance floor, for I fear that those two young men are about to have words over you. I hope it does not result in a row," he snickered. Then he remarked dryly, "I daresay, what a scandal that would cause."

"I fear that you are right, Father, and I do not like it at all."

But before the earl and Margaret could leave the room, Margaret saw Henry stop the duke from heading towards the ballroom.

In a determined tone, Henry proclaimed, "I know what you are about, Witherton. Do not fool yourself into believing I am unaware of what you are trying to do. And let me be the one to *guarantee* you that it will not work. Lady Margaret is mine! I have courted her for years, waited for her to come of age, and she *will* marry me! Do not think for a moment that you can or will change that."

"On my brother's life, you have nothing to fear from me. I truly just enjoy the presence of Lady Margaret."

It sounded sincere, but then, not many people knew that the duke's brother was illegitimate and they were estranged. Henry had told Margaret as much.

"I am not inexperienced. I know how much your word is worth." With that, Henry turned on his heels and brusquely walked over to the earl and Margaret.

"I am sorry you both witnessed that interaction."

"Nonsense, my boy. You will never see me upset over you protecting my daughter."

Margaret refrained from commenting. She abhorred the confrontation between the two men but knew any protest on her part would only make the predicament worse.

The three of them entered the ballroom where all the other guests were already gathered and preparing for the first dance of the evening.

The earl asked Margaret as they approached the edge of the dance floor, "Daughter, would you like to honor me with your first dance?"

She was a bit nervous. She had never danced at a ball before. Yes, she knew how to dance quite well, but that was in theory with her dance instructor. *This* was different. This was in front of hundreds of people who were just waiting for her to misstep or, better yet, trip and fall on her face, so they would have something to gossip about at their next teatime.

"Actually, I was hoping that the Lady Margaret would

give me the honor of her first dance," Henry said earnestly as he reached out his hand to her.

Goodness! How was she going to get out of this? The room almost felt as if it were spinning and a painful knot was forming in the pit of her stomach. She did not think she could manage to stay on her feet the way she was feeling. How could she make excuses to Henry without hurting him further?

"I really do not feel up to it, my lord. If you would allow me to sit out this dance, perhaps I will feel more inclined after a bit."

He stared at her for a moment without shifting his gaze or features, then replied, "As you wish. I shall stay by your side until you feel up to it."

But only moments passed before Henry's aunt, Baroness Wollingleer, came and tapped Henry on the shoulder with her fan, asking him to dance.

And with that, the betrothed couple, knowing that it would be rude to turn down a guest, split ways, Henry replying to the baroness, "I would be honored to dance with you, Lady Helen."

Watching as her fiancé danced with his aunt, Margaret critically studied the older woman who was Henry's godmother. Lady Helen had been the most attractive woman of the ton during her peak, and traces of her exceptional splendor still lingered underneath the aging woman's face. But as her beauty slowly abandoned her over the years and she gained a significant amount of weight, bitterness took root. Her only joy left was being one of the many gossips of the titled.

Margaret was resigning herself to not dancing the first waltz when Richard materialized out of nowhere.

"My lady, I would count it a privilege to be able to dance this first dance with you."

Hesitantly, she thought about the implications of dancing with the duke. She was feeling better and the queasiness had subsided, but she felt torn between upsetting Henry and disrespecting a higher-titled nobleman. Before she could object, she found herself being swept onto the floor and into the arms of the Duke of Witherton.

Clumsily at first, she tried to keep up with the steady movements of the waltz. Then quickly she fell into the pattern her instructor had taught her and it became like second nature.

"You dance well for your first time, Lady Margaret. I cannot help but wonder if you excel at all new things."

She blushed again. She had not blushed so much since she got her "becoming a woman" speech from her nurse. And why did that thought naturally come to mind? Why was it that when he held her, being a woman in every sense of the word seemed to be paramount? And most frighteningly of all, why did part of her secretly want him to be the one to teach her?

"Thank you, Your Grace. I am pleased that you think I dance well."

"You are most graciously welcome. Did I mention that

you look lovely tonight? More so than what I had expected or hoped."

His comment piqued her interest, so she asked, "Why exactly did you come here?"

"Why, to make your acquaintance, of course."

Skeptically, Margaret replied, "Nice attempt at flattery, Your Grace, but I *know* that I am not known outside my county."

"Ah, but you have indeed been mentioned in my circle of acquaintances. And I know a great deal more than you might think."

"Is that so? Then I shall keep that in mind."

They continued to dance, but Margaret could not help but notice Henry watching them intently with a barely concealed affronted demeanor. When the dance ended, Margaret stepped back quickly and curtsied, wanting to distance herself from the man who was too tempting when holding her near his frame. She hated how she already missed his embrace and craved to be wrapped in his arms again.

"Thank you, Your Grace, for the dance."

"It was my honor, I assure you. Perhaps we can dance again before the eve is through."

"I believe that the Lady Margaret's night is *completely* full."

Margaret felt Henry's hand come to rest on her shoulder from behind. She could tell Henry was staking his claim on her and asserting to Richard that she was unavailable in every way that mattered.

But Richard was not dissuaded. "I am sure that the Lady Margaret can make her own choices as to with whom she wants to dance." He looked at Margaret meaningfully. "Another time perhaps."

With a slight nod, the duke left the pair alone.

Henry looked at her for a tense moment before saying with controlled frustration, "I thought you were not feeling well."

"Yes, I was not but after I bit of time passed, I felt much better."

With unmasked irritation this time, he quipped back, "I could see that. You got well fast enough to dance with the duke!"

"I could not very well turn him down, now could I?" Margaret said defensively.

"I see, but you could me," Henry said with rising resentment.

"My lord, you take my words out of context. That is not what I meant."

"Then, by all means, explain."

She stopped for a moment and then, without being able to control it, started to laugh. How silly the two of them must seem! To fight over such nonsense as to who she danced with seemed ridiculous to her. She was engaged to Henry and everyone knew it. There was no competition except what was in Henry's head.

First astonishment, then anger crossed his face. He

started to turn and walk away when she lightly grabbed his arm.

"Henry, stop, do not be angry with me! Please wait. I would love it if you would dance with me."

He stood still for an instant and then turned around. "You have not called me by my given name since we were children, not even upon my insistence."

"I know."

"Then why now?"

"Because, despite what has happened this evening, I had hoped to find a way to be the woman you deserve. I know I am not very good at it, but the truth is, you mean a great deal to me and I want our life together to be happy. I want our future marriage to work, and I will do whatever it takes to make it happen."

For the first time that night, she saw a smile cross his face. "Then I will be more than honored to dance with you, my love."

And for the first time, it did not seem so embarrassing to have Henry call her an endearment.

Henry led Margaret into the center of the ballroom. A fast-paced song began and everyone followed the steps to the Mazurka. Surprisingly, Margaret found herself enjoying their time dancing. He was a good dancer and they chatted pleasantly since they had much in common, but despite her best efforts, her mind continued to drift back to her time with the Duke of Witherton.

After the song ended, Henry escorted Margaret off the

dance floor and over to her father. He excused himself, explaining that one of his servants had come with an urgent business matter he needed to attend to right away. He would only be absent for a few minutes while he gave instruction for what needed to be done.

Margaret smiled and began to patiently wait for her betrothed's return when Henry's uncle, the Baron Wollingleer, approached her. He was a short, portly man who had mastered the art of being excessively uncouth. Margaret avoided him when possible. It seemed she was not going to have the luxury of escaping his presence tonight.

"I believe it is my turn to dance with you, Lady Margaret, since my nephew has left you partner-less. After all, we should get to know each other better since soon you will be my niece."

The lechery tone he used was unmistakable as he talked to her. The baron had a reputation of taking advantage of young girls. She hoped that her being promised to his nephew would keep him from making advances towards her, but knowing all the stories that were whispered about him, she would not put it past him to try.

Margaret reluctantly nodded and put out her gloved hand for him to take. He escorted her onto the dance floor as he gathered her into his arms, a little too closely for Margaret's liking, as the music began.

"I do say, you look quite becoming tonight. My nephew is a *very* fortunate man!"

"Thank you, Lord Marcus, for the acclamation."

"You know, since we will be family soon, it would not be ill-conceived for us to spend some time alone getting to know one another better."

Margaret tried to hide her disgust at his lascivious comment, then replied, "I do not think your nephew, my betrothed, would be very amicable with that idea."

"Come now, you did not seem to mind when the Duke of Witherton was getting to know you alone at the top of the stairs earlier this eve."

So, he had seen her interaction with the duke, which meant his horrid wife, most likely had seen it as well. No doubt, since she was one of the biggest gossips in the ton, Margaret would be fodder for the gossips by night's end.

"He approached me while I was waiting for Henry, and I was merely being polite to one of my guests as any proper young lady should be."

"Say what you might, but I think you are more open to spending time with other men than you are feigning. I am only suggesting that I might be one of your admirers to whom you give special attention."

Margaret stiffened and tried to put some space between them as they danced. She was becoming increasingly uncomfortable with the baron.

"Lord Marcus, I am not feeling myself. Would you please allow me to end our dance that I might be able to sit down?"

A look of displeasure crossed the baron's face as he said, "I think you can manage a little longer, my dear. We are just getting started."

What was she going to do? She could hardly stand to be near him and there was no dignified way to free herself of him without creating a scene. She felt trapped and truly feeling ill at the thought of dancing any longer with the baron.

Suddenly, the duke appeared behind the baron and tapped him on the shoulder, saying, "Baron Wollingleer, I think your time with Lady Margaret has come to an end."

Margaret could see that the baron wanted to argue with him, but as Richard was of higher nobility, he deferred to the duke, saying, "As you wish, Your Grace."

Smoothly sweeping her into his arms for a second time, the duke guided her around the dance floor.

"I hope you do not resent me interrupting, but it seemed as if you could use rescuing from the cad."

"Thank you, Your Grace. I appreciate you intervening. He thinks he has the right to take liberties with me since he is my betrothed's godfather and uncle."

"Nothing gives a man the right to mistreat a lady. Albeit the circumstances, I welcome the chance to dance together again."

Margaret smiled up at him and stated, "As do I, my lord."

"Glad to hear it."

As he spun her around the floor, Margaret felt like she was floating on clouds. Just the mere touch of the duke's hand resting at her waist made her giddy with excitement. He held her just a little closer than was necessary but not enough to create a scandal. She did not want the song to end, as she thought nothing could feel more perfect than being in his arms.

Richard leaned down and whispered, "My lady, I have to confess. I am glad Lord Marcus is a cad since it afforded me the opportunity to be with you again."

"Although I should not admit this, I feel the same way."

He smiled at her and started to reply, but the music ended, cutting off his response. Hesitantly, Margaret curtsied and Richard bowed in return.

"I think it is time I brought you to your father before even more tongues are wagging about us having two dances together this eve." The duke escorted Margaret over to her father and said, "I hope the rest of your evening is everything you hope it will be. Good night, Lord Wellesley, Lady Margaret."

After the duke had left and was out of earshot, the earl turned to Margaret and asked, "What happened to make the duke interrupt your dance with Lord Marcus?"

"The baron was making me feel uncomfortable with the way he was speaking to me. The duke must have seen through my body language how upset I was becoming and chose to intervene."

"I think, given how your betrothed feels about him, it would be best if you avoid future contact with the duke."

Margaret's heart sank at the idea of avoiding Richard. She knew she should agree with what her father wanted for the sake of her engagement, but she found herself intrigued by the duke. She was certain she desired to get to know him better but knew she could not confide that in her father. Instead, she said, "I care about how Henry feels, I truly do, but I cannot ignore someone of the duke's station if he chooses to attend another function here in Brighton. After all, you raised me to be a proper lady."

"Of all the times for you to care about being proper, daughter, this is not one of them. You need to consider what is best for your future husband, and avoiding the duke should be at the top of your list."

"I agree," Margaret heard Henry say behind her back. "You need to stay away from him. I heard from my uncle that the duke interrupted your dance with him. He is trying to irritate me and lure you in at the same time."

"He was nothing but a gentleman and was polite at every moment, which is more than I can say for your uncle."

"My uncle can sometimes speak out of turn, but he is harmless."

Margaret wanted to tell him how the baron had lewdly behaved towards her, but mortification over the entire situation made her remain quiet on the subject.

"I do not want to argue over this, Henry. Can we please just dance together and forget all of this happened tonight?"

He stared at her for a long moment before saying, "Tonight is your night, Margaret. I will do your bidding."

Henry took her by the hand and led her onto the dance floor. She pushed everything else out of her mind and focused on the enjoyment of moving to the music.

CHAPTER 3

With slow ease, Margaret stretched her arms above her head. It had been a long night indeed, full of dancing, laughter, and fun.

Then she thought about the gossip she had overheard. Everyone was talking about how the two most eligible and sought-after young men of the ton were fighting over her. "It was enough to make a person's blood boil!" one of the women had said with a giggle.

Margaret had never liked being the center of attention or the source of gossip, but she had to admit, a small part of her felt delighted to have both Henry and Richard seeking her favor. The problem was that she should not like or accept Richard's attention as she was betrothed to Henry. Her mind knew that, but her heart rebelled.

She knew the answer, of course. Henry. He had always

been there, and no doubt he would be there long after Richard was gone.

"My lady, I have your breakfast here for you. It is your favorite, on your father's orders," her lady's maid, Sarah, stated with a smile.

Looking at the tray expectantly, it looked delicious. Two-minute eggs and toasted bread accompanied with freshly brewed tea and coffee were waiting to be devoured.

"Tell my father that I absolutely adore him and that he is the best father in the world!"

"I will deliver the message, my lady." Sarah stopped and looked at Margaret with big green eyes. "You do remember that you have church service this morning and after, riding with Charlotte's Pride scheduled for the afternoon?"

Religious activities were a routine part of her life. Both her parents had been Christians and had attended religious services regularly. After her mother's death, her father continued to go every Sunday and made sure that she was in attendance as well. She, on the other hand, had a hard time relating to the abstract God that was so prevalent in the sermons that she heard every Sunday. That was one of the things that she and Henry had in common. They both believed in God but viewed God more as someone watching over them and putting his unknown plans into motion. They had talked in length about it growing up, and they both believed God was watching and protecting them but that was the extent of his interaction in their lives. Margaret and

Henry agreed that, if you were a good person and believed in God, that was all God really wanted from you.

"Yes, let me finish my breakfast, and then have one of the servants come help me get ready for the day. Meanwhile, as I finish this—" She took a bite of the blueberry scone. Getting a crumb on her lower lip, she gently dabbed it away with a napkin. "—please prepare my yellow outfit with the cream trim and matching hat for this afternoon and confirm with my father's valet that my father is ready to go. You know how he gets busy with his work and forgets the time."

"Yes, my lady, I will do that right now. I have already laid out your pink dress with the embroidered flowers on it along with its matching hat for church service. If that will be all, my lady, I will be on my way to take care of those tasks."

Margaret watched the departing figure of her companion and, in all reality, only true confidant. Growing up, Margaret was incredibly shy and unable to relate to the other girls her age with whom she was expected to associate. She was different, having an intense desire to read and spend countless hours in the stables. The only person she was able to talk to was Sarah, and due to that, the most unlikely friendship was forged.

Sarah was beautiful when Margaret thought about it. If circumstances had been different and Sarah had been born into a titled family, she could easily have been the center of the ton and won countless hearts. With her long blonde hair and bright green eyes, she was a sharp contrast to Margaret's dark beauty, but that was where their differences ended.

Their personalities, tastes, and principles were almost exactly the same. That was probably why Margaret never found a need to have other acquaintances. All she needed in a friend and companion, she found in Sarah.

But recently, Margaret could feel Sarah distancing herself emotionally from Margaret, almost as if Sarah knew that when Margaret was married, their unusual friendship would have to change to accommodate Margaret's new position in Henry's household. Margaret did not like it but could not figure out a way to fix the growing distance between the two.

As Margaret finished her morning meal, her mind floated to thoughts of her horse, Charlotte's Pride, named after her mother. Her father doted on her, and because of her intense love of horses, he listened to her input in regards to the ones they owned. As her most prized horse, Margaret focused her attention towards making sure that the trainers were doing everything properly to prepare Charlie, as she liked to call her, for show. As a woman, Margaret was not allowed to train or show Charlie herself, but it did not stop her from reading extensively on the subject and spending many hours in the stables soaking up what knowledge she could. Her young Arabian filly was the most magnificent of their estate horses and had consumed her life the past year.

Charlie was pure black from her mane to her tail. The only sign of color was the white blaze on her forehead, a trait passed down through her bloodlines. She was a beautiful horse, and people had already been making offers. Thankfully, when it came to their estate horses, her father took her feelings into consideration. She asked him not to sell Charlie even though he had been offered a small fortune.

Money was of little consequence to Margaret as her father had plenty, and soon she would be married to Henry, whose income was almost twice her father's. Once she was married, she could devote her whole life to her husband, future children, and horses. Until then, Charlotte's Pride would have to do.

Margaret expected to see the regular attendees of their local church. Henry would be there of course, sitting next to his uncle and aunt, the Baron and Baroness Wollingleer, since both his parents were no longer alive. Also present would be the Earl of Bunsdure; the Marquess Sedrick, who was cousins with Queen Victoria; Lord and Lady Almonbury, who lived near Margaret and her father; and various other important people within their county.

When she arrived, Margaret noticed there was a great bit of buzz surrounding Holy Trinity Church. Something was going on that had everyone whispering. As she entered the chapel doors after her father, she saw the faces that belonged, but to her surprise, she glimpsed someone unfamiliar sitting in a place of honor in the front pew. Seeing the back of the man's head, something about him seemed familiar.

The stranger was talking with Reverend Portman as well as the Earl of Bunsdure. He seemed to be exacting the undivided attention of the other two men, as the three were completely absorbed in their conversation.

Margaret followed her father to their place, two pews behind the stranger, and sat down. Pursing her lips, Margaret glanced up and tried to get a better glimpse of the man without making it obvious.

It could not be. She could see the side of his face now, and she realized with shock that it was the Duke of Witherton. Of course, it made sense that he was at church since he had been at the ball last night and most likely stayed with a friend or relative nearby, but it seemed quite curious that he was becoming familiar to everyone in her county so suddenly. What was his motive?

Trying to keep her mind on the sermon to no avail, Margaret continually found her thoughts focusing on the duke. His presence made her uncomfortable, not because she did not want him there, but rather because she did. She should not want to see him or find a reason to talk to him again, but as the service was ending, she realized she was going to come up with an excuse to do just that.

But before Margaret could get out of her pew and make her way up to the duke, Baroness Wollingleer stopped her. "My dear, how are the wedding preparations going?"

Margaret politely replied, "I have not really been thinking about it as the wedding will not be for at least another two years."

It was obvious the answer did not sit well with the baroness. Her plastered smile quickly turned into a disapproving frown.

"But you and Henry have been betrothed for so long What reason is there to wait?"

Margaret was trying to think of a way to answer when Henry stepped in and said, "Aunt Helen, you know Margaret's father and I have made all the arrangements regarding this matter and that we are in agreement that the wedding will take place when Lady Margaret is eighteen."

Smiling at her intended with gratitude, Margaret knew that it was uncommon to wait as long as they had to get married, but Henry had accepted her father's unusual request for them to wait until she was eighteen. The earl had explained that, with Margaret being his only living child and him being a widower, he was not ready to be without her just yet.

"But that seems so old! Why, most girls are getting married at fifteen, or even sixteen at the latest. I want to have some great nieces and nephews before I die."

Henry brought her hand to rest on his arm and patted it, knowing that his aunt could be exasperating. "And you will. The earl just wants to keep his daughter a little longer. You cannot begrudge him that considering the fact that she is all the family he has left."

Changing the subject, the baroness said, "I find it unexpected that the Duke of Witherton came to our church today. I did not even know he attended church while he was in London, let alone when he is on holiday."

Margaret felt Henry's whole body stiffen at the mention of the duke. "I am sure the motives for his time here are nothing but deceitful and vile," Henry warned them.

The baroness raised an eyebrow and scolded benignly, "Henry, you should not talk about someone of his importance that way."

"Aunt Helen, I have much more history with him than I care to discuss, and believe me when I say that he has nothing in his character that is motivated by anything other than revenge and vindictiveness."

"I saw how the duke conducted himself at the ball last night, and I think he might be here looking for a bride," the baroness predicted. "You better keep your eye on this one, Henry, before someone swoops in and takes her off your hands."

Averting her eyes so that neither Henry nor his aunt could see her reaction to her statement, Margaret knew she *should* be offended by what Baroness Wollingleer was saying. But if she allowed herself to admit how she truly felt, she was intoxicated by the idea that Richard might be contemplating wooing her.

After getting her emotions under control, Margaret looked up and casually glanced around, trying to locate the duke.

"Whatever his motives for visiting, I am certain he will be

returning to London shortly and we will no longer have to tolerate his presence," Henry said with eager anticipation.

Margaret's heart lurched. She had not thought about that. How would she feel when Richard returned to London and she never saw him again? She wanted to deny that it would impact her, that his departure would not leave her feeling heartbroken, but as Margaret looked to the side to mask her confused feelings, she saw Richard slowly approaching. Their eyes met and lingered for a split second before he walked past her, and she knew in that instant that she would be devastated if she never saw him again.

But by the time Margaret was able to free herself from Henry's constant presence and search for Richard at the church, it was too late. He had left before she even made it outside. It agitated her that she had not gotten a chance to speak with him, but she kept it masked, knowing that no one would understand.

CHAPTER 4

*H*oping to take her mind off the man who should not be consuming her thoughts, Margaret decided to go for a ride.

Since she cared more about her horses than anything else, Margaret did not conform to the traditional attire a lady wore when riding unless she was with other people from the ton. If she were on her own, she would wear slacks and a blouse and use a standard saddle as opposed to a sidesaddle.

When she had requested her dressmaker to custom design several sets of pants and tops for her riding outfits, he had looked at her like she was foolish. She had to talk him into making them by offering a sizeable payment and explaining that she would only wear the outfits when she was working alone with the horses and no one else would ever see her in them or know he made them for her. Reluctantly, he agreed, but she knew he did not approve.

Today, she was wearing beige slacks with a pale yellow blouse adorned with her mother's cameo, and her hair was pinned up in a French twist.

"Good morning, my darling. How are you today?" she lovingly asked her horse. She felt more comfortable with horses than she did most humans.

Charlie neighed in response and then nuzzled into the curve of her neck. In response, she wrapped her arms around the horse's neck and said, "Thank you for the kiss. You are such a sweet girl. And I have just the treat for you."

Margaret pulled out a lump of sugar from her pocket that she had taken from the kitchen when Cook had not been looking.

Nickering in anticipation, Charlie watched as Margaret put her hand out palm open with the sugar cube sitting temptingly on top. Charlie quickly nibbled up the treat and stomped her hoof in approval.

"I think this morning we will take the back paths towards Burlingler Estate. We've never been in that area, girl, and I feel like exploring."

"My lady, you almost forgot your riding crop," Sarah said as she tried to catch her breath after hurrying to catch up.

"Thank you, Sarah."

"Are you sure, my lady, that you want to ride by yourself? You know I have not been feeling well lately, but I will come along if you need me."

"It is not necessary."

"Yes, my lady, but I fear that it would look terribly

improper if someone were to find you riding by yourself. Do you want me to get one of your other personal servants to accompany you so that we can avoid any gossip?"

"Oh bother. I know all about the ton's rules and standards and how the titled are supposed to act, but that does not mean that I agree with it."

With that, she mounted Charlie and looked at Sarah for a moment, smiling mischievously. Then flippantly, she quipped, "Besides, how much trouble could I really get into?"

"Mistress, do not do anything rash. Your father will have my hide if anything happens to you." Then, almost as an afterthought, Sarah quickly added, "Or worse, you will create a scandal."

"Sarah, you know quite well that scandals do not happen in the country. And for good reason, as there is no one around to witness one being made." And with that, she galloped off towards Burlingler Estate.

It was getting dark and Margaret was getting nervous. She should have been home hours ago. She would not be surprised if her father already had the servants out searching the area for her.

Afraid of the verbal thrashing she knew she would get when she got home, Margaret shuddered. That was all she needed on top of being scared out of her wits. The forest was so thick next to Burlingler Estate that she was lost before she even knew what was happening.

Looking around, Margaret saw a fallen tree nearby. Making her way over to it, she realized it would be as good a place as any to stop for a moment so that Charlie could take a rest. She too needed one, come to think of it.

"It is all right, Charlie. We will find our way home. It is only a matter of getting our bearings." She had said the words to her horse, but realized that she needed to hear them as well.

She had been trying to get her bearings for the last three hours with no luck at all. She was beginning to think it hopeless. But she was not going to give up, and she was not going to give in to the tears that now threatened to escape her carefully controlled demeanor.

Of course, no one was around to see her cry anyway, so what did it matter? How long had it been since she had cried? She thought about it a moment. Then it came to her without her really wanting to remember.

The last time she had cried had been at her brother's memorial. It had been the most difficult day of her life. She had wanted to die as well when they had been informed that her twin brother, Randall, had perished at sea. When they lost Randall, it felt like a part of her had died with him.

She still remembered the denial she went through when the letter had arrived. She insisted that it was not his ship that had sank in a storm but another one like it. He was still going to arrive from boarding school in a few days just like it had been planned. She was going to see him again and place her arms around him and tell him how much she loved him. They would be able to play outside together under the lavender trees and run down to the swimming hole by the river. But those times were never to come again.

"Margaret, dear, you need to rest. Stop waiting by the windowsill for him to return. He is not coming back, and no amount of hoping or wishing is going to change that."

"You are wrong, Father! He is coming home! I can feel it. If he were truly dead, I would know it." She tapped her chest where her heart lay beneath. *"I would feel it!"*

She had held onto that belief, and that was what had kept her from losing her mind. She would not let go of the belief that he was coming home to her. Then the day of the memorial came and all the perfect control she had built up around her came crashing down.

"This is wrong, Father! We cannot be here conducting this service because he is not dead! We are doing something that is absurd and silly. He is going to be coming home any day now and—"

"Daughter, that is quite enough. You are going to stop this right now! Randall is dead, and nothing is going to change that. Let him go. You have to, for the both of us, or we will never get past this."

"You are right. I will never get past this—until he returns to me. And he will! Just you wait, Father. You will see that I am right."

"Margaret, I did not want to have to tell you this, but they found his shirt with his initials on it where the ship sank."

"So, what does that prove? He probably removed it so he could

swim faster to safety." Denial had always come easy to her. When caught in lies when younger, she had denied until her face turned blue that she had anything to do with her and her brother's many antics.

"It was torn up and bloody. The magistrate said that he was quite certain it was his blood and that he was forcibly removed from it by...."

Margaret did not need for him to finish the sentence. She quickly was able to grasp what had happened. They'd believed her twin brother had been attacked by sharks.

"No.... No! He is not dead! He cannot be. I need him so badly," she said in a whimper as she crumpled to the ground in a heaving sob.

In that moment, what had been left of her resolve crumbled. Only the haunting image of her brother being torn apart by sharks as he screamed for help echoed in the back of her mind.

She had nothing to hold on to anymore, and she knew it. The tears came down quickly and harshly, one on top of the other, leaving streaks and trails behind. She did not bother to wipe them away but instead reveled in them—her final connection to the only person who truly understood her and loved her despite all her impish ways.

Realizing over time, she would never forget him as long as she mourned him, she chose never to cry again. She considered her tears a bond between them, and she never wanted to share that bond with anyone else.

But despite her firm determination not to shed tears, she was on the brink of crying.

She sat on the log and hid her face in her hands. What was she going to do? She was frightened and truly had no clue as how to get home.

"What are you doing on Burlingler Estate?" someone said from the shadows.

Startled, she yanked her head up. "Who is there?"

"I should be asking the questions since you happen to be on my land."

She was such a fool. And to think that she had thought it could not get worse. Now she had run into the new owner of Burlingler Estate, and she was trespassing on his property.

Since she overheard the servants discuss how the new owner had recently come to take ownership, she should have known it was a possibility he would be surveying his property. No one knew who he was, but everyone desperately wanted to find out. Now she was going to be the first, but under the worst possible circumstances. Not only was she intruding on his privacy, but she also looked horrible and was without a chaperone. What a nasty scandal this was going to cause!

"If you will forgive me, my lord, I did not mean to intrude."

"Do not lie. If you had not meant to trespass, you would not be here. You fully knew what you were about when you decided to come onto my land."

"I beg your pardon, sir, but I only came here because I have always heard how beautiful it is, and I felt that I would not be disturbing anyone. Please forgive me if I have inconvenienced you." She stood and made her way over to Charlie. "I will be on my way now."

Turning her back to the stranger, she prepared to mount Charlie when a hand grasped her upper arm. She gasped at the infringement on her personal space and froze, going rigid with fright.

Then suddenly, the voice changed somehow and became familiar, saying, "On the contrary, I find it charming that you decided to come visit my land, although next time, you must come visit me at my home instead of getting lost in the woods."

Whirling around, she found herself inches from the Duke of Witherton. "Your Grace, you startled me." She took in his good looks and tried to hide the effect he had on her. He looked magnificent in his chocolate brown slacks and hunter green jacket, and because his curly brown hair was slightly tousled, she wondered if he had just been riding a horse.

She added lamely, "I did not know that you were the new owner of Burlingler Estate."

"Ah, yes, I am full of surprises, if you have not guessed already. This is just one of many." He gestured to the surroundings. "I bought the estate just recently so that I could be closer to my... current interests," he said as he looked at her pointedly.

Understanding his message quite clear, she proclaimed, "How wonderful, for now we are neighbors as well as dancing partners."

"So, little one, you too remember last night quite well."

She certainly did remember their time together. It was scorched into her soul. She had never felt like that before. He made her whole body quiver, and she knew she could not get enough of him.

But not wanting to let him know the truth, she said in deflection, "Yes, it was, after all, my sixteenth birthday."

"And now you are a young woman." He glanced down at her body evocatively. "Did I mention that you look quite fetching this afternoon? That riding outfit enhances your natural beauty perfectly, if that is at all possible."

Not expecting to see anyone when she went riding, Margaret had put little thought into her outfit that day. Subconsciously, she patted at her soft brown and yellow outfit, trying to smooth out the wrinkles she knew must be present.

"Kind of you to flatter me, but I know I must appear a mess."

"I find the sight of you tousled quite appealing." She swallowed hard as he pulled her into his arms and whispered, "Everything about you makes me want more."

Increasingly disturbed by the way he made her feel, Margaret sputtered, "I need to be on my way." She pulled away from him reluctantly, part of her wanting him to pull her back into his arms.

She spun around and mounted Charlie, then started to move towards the way she had come.

"My lady, I hope you do not mind me pointing it out, but you are headed towards my home, not yours." He smiled.

"Not that I mind in the tiniest bit, but your father has the whole area looking for you."

Turning to face him, she trotted Charlie up to where he stood. Then, with all the superior demeanor she did not feel but tried to muster up, she looked down at Richard with fake condescension and replied, "Thank you for informing me, Your Grace, but I was only getting Charlie warmed up before I headed this way."

"Charlie... is not that the horse that the whole country-side is talking about, trying to get a glimpse?"

Sitting up even straighter in the saddle, she replied with satisfaction, "Yes, Charlotte's Pride is my horse and many would like to possess her. She is going to be one of the best show horses in England once she has finished training."

"You daresay? I heard that your family raise some of the finest horses in England. Of all of Europe, some say."

With that, he whistled lightly, and at first, Margaret had no idea why. Then, from the concealment of the shadows, emerged the most beautiful horse she had ever seen. The stallion outshone even her own Charlie.

She took in a deep breath and held it. She stared at the tall, magnificent white horse for several moments and then let out her breath with a sharp gasp. She recognized the stallion from descriptions and paintings. It was one of the Arabian twins! She had heard the rumor that someone in England had bought both of them, but she had no idea who and no one could find out.

Secretly, she had dreamed of one of the twins siring a colt

for Charlie because really, next to her own horses, the twins were the most sought-out and wanted bloodline in Europe. Surely, Richard could not be the new owner because she had never heard that the duke had an interest in horses, especially such a profound and deep interest as to warrant owning the Arabian twins.

"He is beautiful, is he not?"

Nodding in agreement, her eyes grew round in awe. She never thought she would see one of them up close like this. Without thinking, she dismounted and walked over to the famous horse. She reached out to touch him, then thought better of it and pulled her hand back.

"It is all right, you can touch him. He is actually a very gentle horse for all the bad press he has gotten. A lot of the papers have said that he has a horrible temper compared to his brother, but really, he is quite the charmer once you get to know him."

She smiled to herself, catching the double meaning. He was describing himself through his horse. He too had been labeled in the papers as having a bad temper.

Perhaps they were wrong on both accounts. Richard did not seem to have any of the less-than-reputable traits that he had been dubbed with over the years. Maybe the papers just needed someone about which they could gossip.

But then a thought occurred that made her look from the horse to Richard with puzzlement. Reading her expression, he asked, "What is the matter? Did I say something to offend you?"

"No, it just the opposite. It surprises me that you have a love for horses. I have not really known anyone who has as great an interest in them as me." She wanted to say more but finished awkwardly with, "It surprises me, that is all."

"Admit it. What you are trying to say is that you have never met anyone like me, and I always astound you with something new."

She tried to regard him seriously but smiled despite herself. "I will admit no such thing. You are insufferable, sir."

"And you like that as well." He touched the side of her face and turned it towards him. "I intrigue you because you know deep down that I am just like you."

She could not pull away from his touch and, without realizing it, leaned into his hand.

Trying to deny their obvious connection, Margaret said, "That is absurd. We are nothing alike. We come from different worlds."

"So you say, but do you truly think so? I believe that we are very much the same, from our love of horses to our wants and passions." He looked at her with desire, driving home his meaning. "I know what I want."

She began to shake slightly and they both felt it.

Apprehension began to take hold. She should not feel this way, not now and not for him. That was what her mind told her, but her body wanted him to kiss her again. And not on her hand but on her lips this time. What would a real kiss feel like? Would the butterflies come again? Oh, how she ached to find out.

Leaning forward, Margaret sought him without using words. He brushed his lips across her forehead, then trailed light kisses across her brows. She put her hands on his chest and allowed herself to be pulled closer to him. She tilted her face up to meet his lips and felt his mouth descend upon her own.

It was like a jolt of lightning hitting her. Her breath escaped her, and the trembling became unmanageable. She was completely unprepared for this kind of reaction and worried she would faint. What kind of feelings were these?

Quickly, she tore away from his kiss. What was she doing? Why had she let him kiss her? She was such a fool! She had to get away from him.

If anyone caught her here like this with Richard, her reputation would be ruined, not to mention what it would do to Henry. Despite her physical attraction to the duke, she really did want to honor her family's obligation and marry Henry. But if she kept running into the duke like this, how long before she ended up compromising everything she believed in?

Stepping back, she tried to get her ragged breath under control. She turned towards Charlie and mounted hurriedly, almost slipping in her rush. Then, without facing him, she stated, "I have to go. My father must be worried sick."

He moved towards her and stopped next to Charlie's side, putting his hand lightly on the calf of her leg. "Yes, you must hurry home to your father. Oh, and did I forget to mention the Viscount Rolantry is looking for you as well?" Then, with one of his cynical smiles, he added, "Or have you forgotten about him again?"

"No, I have not forgotten about my betrothed." She started to head towards her home when, over her shoulder, she shouted, "Have a good evening, Your Grace, and do try to make it to our wedding."

Margaret had tried to prepare herself for the upcoming questions from her father and Henry, telling herself not to get defensive or it would point directly to the fact that she was covering up some of the truth.

Henry rushed up to her and gently placed his hands on either side of her arms, asking, "Margaret, are you all right? We were worried sick about you!" She heard the concern in his tone, which made her guilt even harder to bear.

"Yes, Henry, I am fine. I got lost in the thicker part of the forest and I could not find my way home."

"Why were you by yourself in the first place?"

"Yes, daughter, do explain why you had no attendant with you."

"Father, I feel that you are making much of an issue out of this. I am sorry that I made you both worry, but as you can see, I am unharmed."

"You are wrong. Your safety is a major issue. It has been too many times that you have put your safety and even life at risk, and this will be the last time. Until you are married to

Henry, I am your guardian and you will not leave this estate without a proper chaperone or ride alone ever again!"

Her father looked at Henry and patted his shoulder. "Good luck, my son. You are going to need it in order to keep her under control."

"Father, I am not a child! You cannot treat me like one." But as she said the words, she realized her indignant tone made her sound exactly like one.

He turned to look at her. "When you act like one, you will be treated as such." He walked over to a table, poured himself a cup of tea and took a drink, keeping the glass in his hand. Tea was the only drink that soothed her father since he had given up drinking after he had gotten married. He had told her that drinking was a vice one could afford when one was young, but a dignified man left foolish ways behind him when he started a family. To this day, she had never seen him partake in libations.

"Henry can do with you as he likes when you are his responsibility, but as long as you are mine, I will see to it that you are unable to participate in any more of your wild escapades." With force, he slammed the glass down, splashing some of the contents over the rim. "I hope that you fully enjoyed this jaunt, because it will be your last!"

There was no point in arguing or denying anything. She knew that when her father got like this, there no reasoning with him, and deep down, she knew it was really her own fault that she was in this predicament.

Why had she been so adamant about going alone? That

was not hard to figure out. Her foolish stubbornness was the root of it all. It always got her into trouble. Despite all her resolve to reform and no longer be willful, she ended up going right back to her old ways.

"Very well, Father. If this is the way you want it to be between us, then this is how it shall remain."

With that, Margaret exited the room, but hearing her betrothed and father continue to talk, she stopped just outside the door to listen, peeking around its edge.

Henry, turning to her father, asked, "Do you think you were too hard on her?"

Shaking his head with a sullen sigh, he replied, "Unfortunately, you can never be overly forceful with Margaret. She never listens to anyone or thinks about the consequences of her actions. She lives in the moment, and almost always, she reaps painful rewards for it." He folded his arms across his chest.

Turning, he looked directly at Henry, saying, "She is the only child I have left and my last connection to my dear Charlotte. Because of that, I indulged her every whim, gave her everything she wanted, and now, I do not know what I am going to with her."

"Do not worry, sir. Soon you will no longer need to worry about her. I promise you that I will protect her and keep her safe, no matter what it takes. I will never let anything happen to your daughter."

CHAPTER 5

$\mathcal{N}$ot looking forward to the formal dinner that the Baron and Baroness Wollingleer were throwing, Margaret tried to prepare herself for the upcoming event. She tried to avoid the insufferable couple as much as possible, as they constantly made coarse comments towards her. They did not believe she gave Henry the amount of attention they felt he deserved and incessantly picked at her because of it.

"Father, are you sure that we have to go tonight?"

"Yes, daughter, we have no choice. We already agreed to attend and they saw us at church yesterday. We must attend their dinner tonight."

Margaret sighed and looked at herself in the entry hall mirror once more before it was time to leave. She was quite pleased with the beautiful lavender dress she was wearing. It was made of the finest muslin and was cinched in at the waist, enhancing her figure. The cap sleeves fluttered upon her delicate shoulders and the bottom of her dress had light tulle underneath that made it puff out beautifully around her. Complementing the gown, she was wearing a gold heart-shaped necklace with matching amethyst earrings. Half her hair was pinned at the crown of her head while the rest of her raven locks cascaded down her back, and dainty flowers were cleverly arranged throughout. She may not be enthusiastic about the upcoming night, but at least she did not have to look like she was not going to enjoy it.

"Are you ready to go?"

"Yes, Father, except can you help me with this?" Her father took her evening cloak and placed it around her, and then they both walked out the front doors of their estate.

On the short carriage ride to the Wollingleer estate, Margaret thought about how she was going to get through the night. The people in the ton were excruciating to be around, and listening to them whine and gossip about the most trivial nonsense was like torture. She would much rather curl up with a pleasant book and read by the fireplace at home.

"You will be on your best behavior this evening, will you not, Margaret?"

"Of course, Father. You know I will not embarrass you."

"I wish I could count on you to hold your tongue, but the last time we were at one of these dinners, you made a very snide comment to the baroness."

"She deserved it! She told me that I needed to cut back on

eating so many scones or I would regret it on my wedding day. All I said in return was that not everyone gains weight as they get older."

The earl snickered and said, "She *has* put on quite a bit of weight over the years and should not be telling anyone how to conduct themselves in that regard."

"I will do my best not to have a similar incident tonight."

"Excellent. Let us just get through this night, and then we can return home. Hopefully, we will not have to attend another one of their dinners for a few months."

Margaret was glad to hear that. She could look forward to a reprieve from the baroness's prying at least for a while. Margaret smiled and was about to say so when they arrived at the Wollingleers' estate.

As the footman helped her down from the carriage, she looked up to see Henry standing at the steps of the front entrance.

He looked atypical in his suit of dark blue. His bow tie was a standard black with matching vest, and he wore his blond hair slicked back per routine. Henry smiled as he walked down the stairs to greet her.

"You look beautiful as usual, Margaret."

"Thank you… Henry." She was still getting used to calling him by his given name. "You look handsome tonight."

"I am glad you could make it. I would not want to be here without you."

Looking at Henry, Margaret said with a small shudder, "It is a bit chilly out this eve. I am glad I wore my thicker cloak."

"Let me get you inside before you turn to ice."

As Henry escorted her inside, the butler took her cloak and beaded clutch, and then Henry guided her into the parlor for drinks and hors d'oeuvres.

Margaret recognized everyone inside. It was the same noble families from the ton that attended all the parties in their small county of Brighton and Hove. It was going to be a boring night indeed.

Lord and Lady Almonbury along with Marquess Sedrick and his new wife, Lady Elizabeth, were in deep conversation. Periodically, they would look over at Henry and Margaret but continued to talk amongst themselves.

Making no effort to converse with them, she did not notice immediately they continued to glance at her as if they were talking about her in particular. She wondered what was going on that had them focusing on her so intently.

The Earl of Bunsdure, who had been talking with another small group of people, walked over to Margaret and Henry and smiled knowingly. "Lady Margaret, so glad to see you. You look lovely tonight."

"Thank you, Lord Bunsdure."

"Did you hear about our surprise guest?"

Margaret widened her eyes and questioned, "To whom are you referring?" She looked around the room and did not see anyone out of place.

"He should be arriving any moment. Baroness Wollingleer wanted to be friendly and invite our new neighbor."

Could it be? It had not even crossed her mind as a possibility, but was it conceivable that Richard was going to be in attendance tonight?

She tried to contain her excitement at the prospect of it. Ever since their encounter in the woods, she had been obsessively thinking about when she would be able to see him again. She felt giddy with hopeful anticipation.

"Ah, here is our new neighbor now," Lord Bunsdure said with a hint of mischief in his voice as he looked over her shoulder.

Turning around, she found herself face-to-face with Richard. She drank in his good looks and could not help but admire the attention to detail he put into his attire. He had on a stunning black suit that had been perfectly tailored to his body. There were hints of silver woven through the material, and his dark burgundy ascot with swirls of gray accents was gracefully tied at his neck. His dark curly brown hair was parted on the side and effortlessly swept across the right side of his forehead.

He looked at her for several seconds before he said, "Good evening, Lady Margaret," and then, almost as an afterthought, he acknowledged the men standing next to her, "Lord Bunsdure, Rolantry."

Staring at him, Margaret waited for him to show some sign of affection. But before anything could occur, Lady Helen entered the room and announced, "Everyone, it is time for dinner. Please make your way into the dining hall."

As they entered the room, everyone made their way

around the table to find their places. At the end of one side of the table, next to the baroness, Margaret found her name. Henry was assigned to sit across from her, and to Margaret's surprise, Richard had been placed next to her. She realized that she had been set up by the baroness to see if she could entrap Margaret with the seating arrangement.

The duke picked up his card and looked at it with a smirk. "It seems that our hostess wishes for us to get to know one another better."

Margaret looked up at Richard with unease evident in her eyes and whispered only loud enough for him to hear, "The baroness is always up to something."

He chuckled under his breath and then said softly, "Come now, do not pretend to be unhappy about this. We both know that you want to be near me as much as I want to be near you."

"Even if that were true, it is not proper."

"When has being proper ever stopped you from going after what you want?"

He was right. It had not stopped her from letting him kiss her in the woods or from enjoying how it made her feel. If she let herself admit it, she was quite pleased that the baroness has placed them next to each other. The problem was that she should not be pleased with the situation. She was treading on dangerous ground, allowing herself to be this close to him with so many people around. If she was not extremely careful, someone was bound to see her reaction to him.

"Here, let me help you with your chair, Lady Margaret." Richard pulled her chair out from the table and firmly placed his hand under her elbow, guiding her into her seat.

It was as if his mere touch seared her, causing her skin to tingle where his hand had lingered just a moment longer than was necessary. He was teasing her with his touch and he knew it. He was teasing her and she liked it.

"Thank you, Your Grace."

"My pleasure."

Richard sat in his seat next to her. "I am glad I was invited tonight. It seems Brighton is becoming a place I quite enjoy."

Henry stared across the table at them, and Margaret could feel his anger boiling under his cool demeanor.

"I think you should return to London, Lord Townsend, where you belong."

"You did not hear, Rolantry? I bought Burlingler Estate, right next to your fiancée's home. I find country life suits me quite well. I do not think I will be going back to London anytime in the near future."

Before Henry could respond, the servers came out and began to serve the first course of the meal.

The evening went by far more quickly than Margaret would have liked. She found herself having to hide her enjoyment of Richard's companionship during dinner since Henry never took his eyes off them.

The other dinner guests started to stand up to leave, but Richard and Margaret delayed getting up, causing them to be the last guests at the table. Richard whispered to Margaret,

"If you decide to go riding again, you could make sure that your servants know where you are going and we might be able to have a repeat of our last encounter."

Looking at Richard, she replied, "Our last encounter cost me dearly. I am not allowed to leave the grounds without someone accompanying me now."

"You are very capable. If you are determined, you will find a way."

Their conversation was interrupted when Margaret's father came to fetch her to leave.

As they headed out the door, her father said, "Daughter, you spent too much of tonight focusing on the duke when you should have been paying more attention to your betrothed. He left a few minutes ago and did not look happy. You better be careful or you are going to throw your future away on a man who looks at you as a passing fancy."

Margaret had not realized that Henry had left already. The truth was she *had* been completely absorbed in Richard and had paid little attention to much else that night. She did not want to hurt Henry, but her feelings for Richard were deepening. What was she going to do? Her heart wanted to pursue what was forming with Richard, but her head told her she would be ruined if she tried to break her commitment to Henry. She felt trapped between what she wanted for herself and the future her father had chosen for her. She did not know what she was going to do.

CHAPTER 6

*M*argaret intended to follow her father's instructions regarding an escort for her afternoon ride. Of course, she planned to take a servant of her choosing whom she knew she could trust and would not try to control what she did.

As she headed to her father's study, she heard laughter coming from the room. Who was in there with her father? She did not know anyone was expected to be here for business. She peeked through the crack of the doors and saw a man sitting in a chair facing her father with his back towards the doors.

"What you are saying is nothing has changed in regards to Lady Margaret's betrothal? She remains engaged to the Viscount Rolantry?" The other man had a thick French accent that sounded familiar, but Margaret could not place it.

"I know that you have been interested in my daughter for some time now, Pierre, but you are quite right. She is spoken for, and I will not be changing my mind on that accord."

Pierre? Oh, now she knew who was visiting—it was Pierre Girard, the Vidame of Demoulin. He had just inherited his title from his father and must be tying up loose ends on his father's previous business endeavors.

Their families had been friends for years, and his family had come to visit three years ago. They had spent the summer playing together while their fathers conducted business. Pierre was two years her senior and had grown enamored with her. Henry had become territorial, as always, making sure they did not have a moment alone together. She was surprised that she had made such an impact all those years ago that he was still interested in knowing her marital status.

"I am guessing that her moving to Paris if she were to marry me also plays a significant measure in your decision making."

"Well, yes, undoubtedly, I would want her to remain close to home."

"What if I were to guarantee that she would be allowed to travel freely from France to England?"

"That is very generous of you, Pierre, but I also must refuse your request because of my promise to the previous Viscount Rolantry. I made him a promise and I will keep it no matter what offers are made. I owe him at least that much for all he did for me when we were young."

Why was her father so determined to keep her engaged to Henry? Every time any man showed an interest in courting her, her father refused to entertain the idea. Not that she wanted to be with Pierre. He had always been kind and he was pleasant to look at with jet-black hair and dark eyes, but she could not keep her mind from constantly straying to Richard.

Shaking his head in disappointment, Pierre said, "I suppose we should discuss other matters since there are no concessions regarding your daughter. In regards to the land purchase you and my father had been negotiating before his death, I will continue to invest the same amount and wish to maintain the same equity for the new hospital that will be built in London."

"Certainly, Pierre. I had assumed as much and am glad to have it confirmed."

The French nobleman stood and shook the earl's hand, saying, "Lord Wellesley, thank you for your time. I am grateful for you seeing me on such short notice. I was in the area on other business and felt I would like to discuss the previous matter in person, considering its delicate nature."

The earl and Pierre made their way over to the doors as Margaret's father said, "Indeed, it was good to see you, Lord Girard."

Margaret quickly leaped back as they approached and raised her hand as if she were about to knock. As her father opened the door, he looked startled to see her on the other side.

"What are you doing here, daughter?"

Glancing up at Pierre, she noticed that he was staring at her knowingly, as if he suspected she had been eavesdropping at the door.

Averting her eyes from Pierre's probing gaze, Margaret turned her attention to her father. "I was coming to tell you that I am headed to the stables as I am going for my afternoon ride, Father. And do not worry, for I am taking one of the servants with me just like you asked."

"I am glad you are listening to me and doing what a fitting young lady should."

Margaret blushed, embarrassed that he would point out one of her flaws with a gentleman in the room.

"Father, you know I try to please you."

"Yes, and I know it often goes against your core nature."

She flinched internally, hurt that her father thought so little of her character, but wanting to get away and see the duke, she smiled dotingly and bit back her response.

"I can escort the Lady Margaret to the stables, Lord Wellesley." The earl furrowed his eyebrows together in contemplation, and before he could reject his offer, Pierre added, "With one of your servants as a chaperone, of course."

Reluctantly, the earl nodded his approval and said, "Since you are old friends, I suppose allowing you to reacquaint yourselves would be acceptable."

"Thank you, Lord Wellesley. I will take good care of her," Pierre said as he gently placed his hand under Margaret's elbow.

64

After her father was far enough away not to hear their conversation, Margaret said, "I am able to go to the stables on my own. I do not need to take up your time. You may go, my lord."

"On the contrary, I would be pleased to spend time with you, Lady Margaret."

Frustrated but trying to disguise it, Margaret said tartly, "I am not sure why you insist on going with me. As I am certain you are aware, I am spoken for, my lord."

He winked at her and asked, "Were you listening at the door to my conversation with your father?"

Indignant, she countered, "I have no idea to what you are referring."

He laughed lightly and said, "Come now, your secret would be safe with me. I believe I saw your shadow depart from the door as we approached."

"You are mistaken. I did no such thing."

"As you wish, keep your secrets to yourself, but your father expects me to escort you to the stables, and so I will. You will be gone from me soon enough."

Realizing she was not getting anywhere with Pierre, she grudgingly allowed him to guide her out of the house and into the back gardens.

"I see you have not changed, my lord. You are exactly the same."

He scoffed. "You are mistaken. I am much more aware of what the world has to offer, which has made abundantly clear to me what I want," he said pointedly as he looked at her.

"I think you have grown bolder, sir."

Ignoring her chastisement, he said, "You have only grown more lovely, Lady Margaret, which is hard to imagine possible. I see you have kept your independent streak as well, judging from your attire."

Margaret glanced down at her outfit and realized that she was wearing one of her riding pantsuits. Flushed with embarrassment, she stated, "I did not plan on seeing anyone before my ride."

He laughed, "You should not worry. You look just as enticing as ever."

"No one is supposed to see me like this."

"I thought we already established that your secrets are safe around me."

"Thank you for being discreet, my lord."

"I fear you have me at a disadvantage, as I never stopped thinking about you."

Margaret's mouth fell open at the sheer bluntness of his statement. She knew men had asked to court her, but it still surprised her how men could act even when they knew a woman was unavailable.

"You flatter me, sir, but you must not say such things to me. You are being entirely inappropriate."

He snickered. "It would not be the first time, and I daresay it will not be the last."

As they arrived at the stables, Margaret tried to pull free from the vidame's grasp, but he would not let her go.

"I think I should take you all the way into the stall of your horse. I wish to be thorough when in regards to you."

Why did everything that came out of his mouth sound evocative? She should not like it, but she found his flirtation stirring something inside her. She needed to get away from him before he became aware of his effect on her.

But before she could extract herself from his presence, he asked, "Is that mare yours?"

Margaret nodded and looked at Charlie. Her pride over her most prized horse superseded her desire to flee his company.

"Yes, her name is Charlotte's Pride."

"She is exquisite! You know, I think I have heard of her. Is she not from a rare bloodline? I am an expert when it comes to horse flesh." Pierre leaned in just past what was decent between two unmarried people and whispered, "Would you like me to go *riding* with you, my lady?" The way he said it, she knew the invitation was for *more* than riding once they were alone. Part of her was tempted to take him up on his offer, but she already had too many mixed emotions from her complicated relationships with Richard and Henry. She was not about to introduce a third man into the equation.

Trying to dissuade him, and herself if she were being honest, she replied in a clipped tone, "That will not be necessary. I much prefer to ride by myself."

"Do you? How provocative."

Blushing, Margaret responded, "My lord, I find this conversation completely unfitting. I believe our time together has come to an end."

"If you ever change your mind, Lady Margaret, I will always be available to be of service."

With that, Margaret turned and headed into the stables, not wanting to respond to Pierre. He made her uncomfortable in a way that she did not understand nor want to explore.

Margaret waited for the stable boy to saddle Charlie. Once he was finished, she patted the horse on the neck and fed her the sugar cube she had in her riding pants. She was mounting Charlie when her youngest personal servant, Francisca, approached her. "I am here, Lady Margaret."

Margaret looked over at the twelve-year-old girl who had long brown hair and matching almond-shaped brown eyes. She was stick thin and had a tomboyish demeanor, which made her perfect for taking on her afternoon rides.

Francisca's mother had been a gypsy, and the earl had taken the girl in as a servant when her mother could no longer take care of her. Since she had no other family, the girl was extremely loyal to Margaret, making her the ideal companion when Sarah was unable to accompany her.

Normally, Sarah went everywhere with Margaret, but Sarah had been feeling sick off and on for the past few weeks and Margaret had gone several days without riding. She was itching to go out, and she knew Charlie wanted to run free. Even though all the horses got daily exercise by the stable hands, Charlie enjoyed galloping in the open countryside.

"Are you ready to go riding with Charlie and me? I had Phillip saddle up one of the horses for you."

Francisca smiled and replied, "As you wish, my lady."

With ease, Francisca mounted the mare and looked at her mistress for direction.

Extra loudly, Margaret stated, "I think we will take the east paths today."

Secretly, Margaret acknowledged that she was purposely taking the paths closest to Burlingler Estate, hoping that she might encounter Richard since he had implied he would find her if she went riding again. It had been a few days since she had seen him at the Wollingleer dinner party, and she hated to admit it but she was desperate to see him again. She knew she should not feel this way, but the more time she spent away from him, the more she knew she was developing strong feelings for him.

"Of course, my lady," Francisca responded.

As they headed out, Margaret smiled and hoped that one of her servants overheard her plans and would relay the information to one of the duke's servants. Hopefully, today would be the day that servants' gossip would pay off in her favor and Richard would know exactly where to find her.

~

Being out for almost two hours, Margaret would have to return soon or face her father's wrath. Disappointment was setting in as she began to accept that she was not going to be seeing Richard.

"My lady, the sun is starting to set. We best be getting back home."

"I am aware, Francisca. I just want to spend a few more minutes and head over to that grove of trees near the small pond. We can let the horses rest for a bit, and then we can head back."

Francisca nodded in agreement.

The two girls reached the grove of trees and brought their horses to a halt. After dismounting, Margaret handed her reins over to Francisca.

"I think I am going to go for a small walk. Stay here and make sure both horses drink plenty of water."

"Yes, my lady."

Walking along the tree line, she looked out towards Burlingler Estate. Where was he? She was so sure she had heard him right when they were at dinner. She really believed her plan was going to work, but he was nowhere to be found.

What was Richard doing at that moment? She hoped he was thinking of her as much as she was thinking about him. She knew her thoughts should not be consumed by him, but the truth was she could not help herself. Every time she tried to stop thinking about him, she would remember their stolen kiss in the woods and she would be wrapped up in thoughts of all the things she wanted him to teach her.

Lost in contemplation, Margaret rubbed her fingertips over her lips as she continued to stroll along the path. She longed to feel his kiss again. There was nothing more in the world she would rather feel.

"Thinking of me, little one?"

Margaret swirled around and found Richard coming from the woods on his estate.

"I was wondering if you would find me, my lord."

"I think, by now, you should be calling me by my given name."

"As you wish, Richard, and you should do the same with me."

Confidently, he smiled at her. "I implied the other night that I have ears everywhere. I was informed that you were taking the east paths, which I knew were between our estates. I am glad you decided to take the risk to come out here considering the restrictions your father has put you under."

"I had hoped you would be as resourceful as I thought you were."

"In other words, you wanted me to find you?"

She nodded. "I had to see you, Richard."

"Why?"

Margaret was afraid to be vulnerable and let him know how she truly felt. What if he did not feel the same? What if she intrigued him but that was as far as it went for him? She did not know if she could take that kind of rejection, especially from him.

Richard closed the gap between them and firmly pulled her into his arms. "I asked you a question, Margaret. Why did you have to see me?"

She tried to focus on his question but was distracted by her body's reaction to him. Her heart attempted to jump out of her chest just from his touch. He smelt amazing, and she relished in feeling his arms around her. Everything about him made her want more.

Finally, she replied, "Because you consume my thoughts."

He looked down at her without saying a word, and for a moment, Margaret was worried he did not feel the same. But as she stared into his eyes, she knew he did.

Slowly, he lowered his lips to hers and demanded her mouth with his own. His hands slid up her back until they were immersed in her hair, and he pulled her even closer, deepening the kiss until she could barely breathe.

He pulled back to say, "From the moment I saw you, I knew that you were the one."

Margaret smiled at him and asked, "What are we going to do about this? I am betrothed to someone else, but I cannot marry anyone else when I feel this way about you."

"I am going to take care of it. Nothing is going to keep us apart."

"I do not want to leave you, Richard, but I have been gone

far too long. If I do not get back soon, my father will be suspicious."

"Yes, I understand, but we will not be apart for long. That I promise you."

Reluctantly, Margaret pulled away and started to head back to where she had left Francisca.

CHAPTER 7

*T*he approaching carriage could be heard before it arrived. The echoing of the horses' feet thudded to a stop outside the main door. Who was it and why were they coming here? Margaret crept up to the corner of the stairs and peeked around to watch the mysterious guest arrive.

She had heard the servants gossiping that it was another suitor, and secretly she hoped it might be Richard. There was no one left unless it was someone from out of town.

Impatiently, she waited for the door to open, fidgeting with anticipation. Petulantly, she snapped in her mind, *Hurry up, sir! I am waiting to see who you are.* The not knowing was driving her mad.

Then, as quickly as her heart was beating in expectation, *he* entered the room, and she thought her heart was going to stop beating altogether. She gasped in surprise, excitement, and fear all mixed together.

It was Richard! He looked incredible in his elegant day suit of navy. He did not seem nervous, which surprised her. Of course, he probably did not know the uphill battle he was going to have to convince her father to let him marry her.

"Your Grace, welcome to Davenmere. The Earl of Renwick will see you in a moment."

With that, both Margaret from her hiding place and Richard from the door watched the old butler retreat to a side door and vanish.

Staring at him for several seconds, she delighted in his magnificent looks. He was so strikingly handsome that it was slightly disturbing. Some said that the devil was the most beautiful of all the angels—was Richard to be her temptation?

She watched him look around and slowly take in his surroundings. Even with no one around him, he did not seem at all worried or irritated to be kept waiting. In truth, no feelings at all were displayed, other than a stance that could only be construed as confident.

What was he thinking? Was he thinking of her, or perhaps the last time they had seen each other? It had only been one day since he had touched her, kissed her, but it felt like an eternity. She had desperately fought the urge to go riding again today, but Richard had said he was going to take care of it, so she had waited. It had been the most difficult thing she had ever done since she wanted to be with him so terribly. It unnerved her how much she craved him.

From around the corner of the bottom of the stairs, Albert, their butler, returned to the duke. "Your Grace, my lord will see you now."

Margaret watched as the departing figures made their way to her father's study. Once she heard the click of the door shutting, she quietly tiptoed down the stairs and over to the study's door. She leaned against it, peeking through the crevice, and listened to the conversation that was already underway.

"I think we both know that horses are not the real reason that I am here, Lord Wellesley. Sir, I have come here to ask for your daughter's hand in marriage. I have come to the conclusion that she is the only one I want, and I feel that she also would find the arrangement agreeable."

"You are exceptionally bold, Your Grace, coming here and proposing marriage to a young lady who is already happily betrothed."

"You are most right, my lord, but you see—I had not planned on admitting this—but I am smitten with your daughter. In all truth, I find myself enraptured when she is present." He stared at the earl for a long moment, and when he did not receive a response, he continued, "As for the Viscount Rolantry, he will have no problem finding another woman to fit his needs. Besides, it is common knowledge that your daughter does not really want to wed him but is doing so out of obligation to you and he continues to stay betrothed also out of duty. I have heard as much from him when we were in the service. He has never looked forward to this upcoming marriage, and I believe it will please all parties concerned if you accept my proposal."

"Yes, but a man is only as good as his word, and I have promised Henry my daughter's hand." The earl thought for a moment in silence, then continued. "Perhaps if we discuss this with Henry—"

"No! I mean, he will only say what he thinks you want him to say. No, think about it. Is not your daughter's happiness your utmost concern? I will be able to offer her a title and wealth unmeasured by anyone else. I know that you made the betrothal agreement before you came in to your current title. You thought at the time that the viscount would be the best that you could do by your daughter, but things have changed, and now I can offer her more than you had ever hoped for, and so can you, by giving me your blessing."

Agonizing moments passed for both Richard and Margaret before finally her father replied, "I am sorry, Your Grace, but my word means more to me than any potential windfall of money and title my family would gain if my daughter were to wed you. She will marry Henry and that is final."

"My lord—"

She did not know what came over her or why she did it, but suddenly she found herself bursting into the room, saying quickly and without thought to the consequences, "Father, do you not wish to hear what I want?"

"Daughter, this is of no concern to you."

"Of no concern to me? I am the one who will be sharing my life with my future husband and bearing his children. Do I not have a right to voice my opinion, for it is I who knows what will make me happy?"

"And what might that be, daughter?"

Angling herself to look at Richard, she replied with deep emotion, "The Duke of Witherton."

The silence in the room was thick.

She looked from Richard to meet her father's eyes, and the mixture of pain and rage she saw there nearly scared her to death. She averted her eyes and walked with her head high over to where the duke stood. Boldly, making her point clear, she took the duke's hand in her own. He did not pull away but instead gripped it back.

"Father, I want to marry Richard and he wants to marry me. Can you not let us be happy?" She looked at him once more and begged with her eyes for him to agree.

"Daughter, you know I would do almost anything for you... but not this. My word is final. I cannot agree to this marriage you claim to want."

"Father, you cannot do this! I demand that you—"

"Margaret, that is enough," the duke said as he looked at the older man. "I will finish this with the earl."

"But I—"

He turned to face her and put his hands on her shoulders. Then low enough for only her to hear, he said, "I will make this happen. No matter what it takes, you and I will be together. I give you my word."

"Richard, I... I...." There was so much she wanted to say, but she did not know how to put it all into words.

"I know. Now hush and be on your way. I will take care of everything."

After a moment's hesitation, Margaret left the room and headed for her own chambers, not wanting to hear the inevitable decision she knew her father would make.

Her father had said no. He had refused every visit and letter the duke made. He would not even allow her outside for fear that they would encounter one another. She was virtually a prisoner. But what was worse was that it stemmed much further than just physically being kept locked up; emotionally she was the same. She was captive to her love for Richard, and she saw no way of her getting free of it or being able to express it openly.

Everything was so horrible. Not only was she miserable, but she had hurt Henry as well. She had known at the time that it would only be a matter of hours before the servants' gossip got to Brookehaven and Henry would find out what had transpired between Richard and her father.

Henry entered through the back, like he had for as long as she could remember. She had been heading up to her room to read when Henry approached her at the bottom of the double staircases.

Margaret thought she had readied herself for the confrontation, but nothing prepared her for the awful truth or the look of resentment and pain she saw on his face.

"Henry, what are you doing here?"

"Do not play coy with me, my lady. You know why I am here." He gritted his teeth as he spit out in bitterness. "How was it so easy for you to trample my heart? Did it mean so little to you? I handed it over to you on a silver platter, but instead of cherishing it, you cut it up and served it to Witherton."

"That is not what happened," she stated, but she knew that it must feel that way to Henry. She did not like the pain that was plainly visible on Henry's face, nor the fact that she was the one who put it there.

Nevertheless, she needed to be honest with him. "I am sorry, Henry, but I cannot deny how I feel. You know all those things that I said I never felt for you and you told me not to worry about it, but I feel them now... with Richard. I did not seek to hurt you, and I wish that this did not, but I cannot change what has happened or my feelings."

"Was everything a lie? You told me you loved me. Did you?" He grabbed her arms and shook her. "Did you? Tell me, did you play with me like a puppet on a string? Have you and Witherton been laughing behind my back about how I have made a fool of myself over you?"

"No! No, that is not how it is. It just happened. I do not

even know how it came to be. One moment, I had resolved myself to marry you, and the next, he consumed my thoughts and feelings."

He pulled away as if she had slapped him. She could see the tears he was fighting back in the corners of his eyes. She hated that she was hurting him this way. He had always been so kind to her, and she cared for him deeply, but she was not willing to lie to him to make this easier.

"Did you ever even really care, or was it all a ruse to wait for something better to come along?"

"That is so untrue, Henry. I care a great deal about you. I loved you. I still do, but I do not think it is the love that a wife feels for a husband. That is what scares me."

Turning away from her, all she could see was the slump of his back. "Do you feel that way about him?"

"Yes, undeniably yes. He makes me feel things that I have never felt before, things I never thought possible."

"What do you want me to say? I know what you want, and yet, I cannot force myself to free you. You have been everything I have ever wanted in life. I cannot see my life without you in it, without you being my wife."

"Henry, you mean so much to me. I also cannot see my life without you in it. My earliest memories have you in them. You and my father have been my whole world ever since my brother died, but now, things have changed and it cannot go back to the way it used to be." Swallowing the newly formed lump in her throat, she forced out, "I want Richard to be my life now."

Moments passed and she continued to stare at his back. Margaret wanted to comfort Henry but realized nothing could make this easier. There was nothing she could say or do that was going to lessen his loss.

"Then I give you your freedom, Margaret, for it is the only thing I have left to give you that you want. You no longer need to consider yourself betrothed to me." She could hear the crushing ache in his voice, and she started to reach out to grab him and keep him from leaving, but put her hand down without saying a word. It was better this way.

Pausing momentarily at the front doors, Henry turned around and looked at her. "My biggest fear is that you will realize too late that he doesn't love you the way you think he does. He is diabolical and selfish, and he will stop at nothing to destroy me, including using you."

"He may have been that way years ago when you were in the military with him, but he has never been anything but caring and considerate with me."

Shaking his head in disbelief, he stated with raw passion so clear in his voice, "I really do love you, Margaret. More than you will ever know, I am afraid." And with those final words, she watched her oldest friend walk through the door, shutting it behind him without looking back.

Margaret had not talked to Henry since he had ended the betrothal. It had only been yesterday, but it felt so much longer. She had not realized until he walked away that not only was he her oldest friend, but he was also her best friend. They had spent countless afternoons together riding horses, taking walks, going on picnics, or playing cards. Even though she had not been in love with him, she had loved spending time with him, and now all of that was at an end. She had not realized how much it was going to hurt to lose him.

"Daughter, I need to talk to you."

She was sitting at her windowsill, staring out, trying to find some way to make sense of the spiraling mess her world had become. She concentrated on the outside, seeking anything that would give her hope for her future.

Turning from the window, she faced the earl. "Yes, Father, what is it?"

"I talked to Henry early today, and he told me about the conversation that took place between the two of you. He told me how he relinquished his claim to you. But the truth of the matter is that the betrothal was not between him and you, but between his father and me. Therefore, since his father is dead, I am the only one who can break this contract."

She was beginning to see where this was going and did not like it at all. Slowly standing up, she narrowed her eyes at him.

"You will still marry Henry. You may not understand now, but you will in time. You are meant for each other. Whether you see it or not at this precise moment, it is so."

"I cannot, Father! Not only am I in love with another

man, but Henry would never want to marry me after all of this. Do you not see that?"

"One would think so, but remarkably, it is just the opposite. As I said, I talked to Henry this morning, and he said that he still loves you and would still be willing to marry you."

"Still willing to marry me? Do you hear yourself, Father? It is an obligation to him. Too much damage has been done to be repaired."

He waved off her appeal. "You are young and have no idea how life really works yet. You are infatuated with the duke. It will pass and Henry will still be there. Henry and I talked of this matter a great deal, and we both believe that these feelings you claim to have will pass in time."

She balled her hands into fists at her side. It took every inch of her self-control to fight back her rising anger.

"I love Richard, Father. I know that as I know my own soul."

"You talk of nonsense. You have no idea what love is or what the traits of true love are."

"Then by all means, Father, share them with me," Margaret said sarcastically. Then, with doubt, she asked, "What makes love *love*?"

While looking at her, he shook his head. "You are so young, daughter, but then I met your mother when she was your age. I knew the moment I saw her that I wanted to marry her, but that was only the beginning. I want you to recognize that love is not self-serving or conceited. It does not remember our iniquities or think evil thoughts of others. Love is gracious and honest. It can withstand anything and always bears hope. If you could grasp these aspects, you would realize that Richard does not embody them."

"Father, you have studied the scriptures and I know you want me to understand the realities of love, but I have never met the man who exemplifies those traits, not even you."

"I know, but I strive to be them, daughter, and that is what I see in Henry. He also will strive to be those things for you. You see, love is not only a feeling but an action. Even when your heart does not feel like loving, you act it out. Emotions are fickle, and one moment you feel one way, and the next you feel completely different. But true love will act and trust that the heart will follow behind. I see this in Henry, and I fear that I do not see this in the duke."

She thought about that a moment, then, with her usual stubbornness, refused to let it penetrate her own beliefs.

"You know my feelings, Father, and what I want. But we both know that in the end, I will bow to your wishes because I have no other choice but to do so."

"In time, my daughter, you will see that I am right. I only want what is best for you. One day, I will not be here, and I want to know that the man you marry will love you and take care of you no matter what."

"I wish you loved me enough to let me make my own choices."

"I love you enough to do the right thing for you, even if it means you end up hating me for it."

CHAPTER 8

*T*wo weeks had passed since her father informed her that she was to still marry Henry. He chose to move up the wedding date to secure the deed was done promptly.

It was her wedding day. By all rights, she should be overjoyed, but here she was about to cry. And they were not tears of joy but of pure distress.

She did not want to walk down that aisle and vow before God, family, and friends that she was going to love, honor, and cherish Henry for the rest of her life. Oh, she would make the promise, but her heart would never belong to anyone but Richard. She kept hoping for a miracle to happen, anything to change what was about to take place.

There was nowhere to turn and nothing to save her from her plight. She had begged, pleaded, and threw herself upon her father's mercy, and yet, he was determined to have this carried out.

What puzzled her most was that Henry still wanted to marry her. Why? She had rejected him, fallen in love with his bitter enemy, and felt no remorse for any of her actions. Yet, on the other side of the door, down the aisle, he was waiting to make her his wife.

Feeling a tear at the corner of her eye, she quickly wiped at it. She was not going to cry. She had faced worse things in her life, and she was not going to cry over this.

Pulling herself together, she stood straight with pride. She was not going to bow, now or ever, because of the injustices life brought her way. She was going to get through this and somehow it would get better.

She reminded herself that her tears were saved for Randall. Her brother's death, seven years ago, had not just been hard on her; it had destroyed her father as well. He refused even now to talk about his lost son.

When they had gotten the letter telling them of his death, she had thought it was a letter saying there was a delay in his coming home for a visit. Instead it told them that he was never coming home again. Her brother had been lost at sea and was presumed dead. The ship that was supposed to bring him back home had gone down in a horrible storm off the coast of France.

At first, she had not cried because she did not believe the news. She remembered telling herself, *My brother is not dead. He is going to be coming home to me any day now. I just know it.*

That was the first time she had sat on the windowsill, looking out in search of something that could give her hope. She stared out over the ocean, hoping against all hope to see his ship on the horizon. For days, she clung to her belief that he had not gone down with the ship as she sat by the window, waiting for him to arrive, hoping against all odds that he would come up the drive in a carriage, hop out, and wrap her in his arms in one of his safe and caring embraces.

And it was in that precise place where her father found her the day of her brother's memorial.

He moved over to her, saying, "You should get ready for the memorial, Margaret."

She did not respond but continued to stare out the window, waiting for some sign to make everything all right again.

Somberly her father pleaded, "Margaret, we need to leave soon. Please, get dressed."

Glaring at him, she snapped, "I need to do no such thing! He is coming back, and I am going to be here to see him when he does."

"He is dead, Margaret, and there is nothing we can do about that. We can honor him by being strong, but you need to let go of this false hope, for both our sakes. Because if you do not, neither one of us will be able to get past this."

She ran up to her father and started to pound on his chest, screaming at the top of her lungs, "He is coming back! He cannot leave me! I already lost Mother. Not him too!" Collapsing into her father's arms, she sobbed, "I need him so terribly, Father. He has always watched out for me and been there. What will I do without him?"

He pulled her tightly into his arms and patted her on the back, holding her for several moments before saying, "We will get through this, my girl, and we will be all right. I love him too, you know. But we have to let him go."

She continued to cry hysterically, and finally after some time, said, "I know... and I will let go. I just cannot believe that Randall is really dead."

Margaret had made a promise to herself and her brother after that day that she would never cry again. Her tears would be her bond between them. She would not break that promise now by crying for her own lost life. She would not allow anything or anyone else to be a part of that connection.

Moving to the nearby mirror, Margaret critically examined herself. She was frightfully pale. Her skin stood out in stark contrast against her dark features. Her paleness was the one small sign that showed her distress, but other than that, she seemed to be the vision of an angelic bride.

Hoping she had applied enough powder to hide the dark circles under her eyes, she added a few more pats for good measure. She hoped when she pulled down her veil, it would discreetly cover the evident distress on her face.

Her hair was artfully arranged around her face, and her dark violet eyes were clear and bright from the unshed tears she had been holding back since this whole thing began. Even so, the paleness made her features stand out even more, and she had to admit that it made her extraordinarily beautiful.

Margaret's wedding gown was of the softest silk, and tiny iridescent crystals were sewn throughout. Her veil was made of the finest ivory lace, complementing her gown perfectly. Its many layers flowed down the back of her, cascading over the train of her dress, which poured out behind her and filled the entry hall. The dressmaker had created a remarkable piece, and every detail had been remembered. But not even the ideal dress could make this day more bearable.

She pushed at the folds of her gown, smoothing out creases and fluffing here and there, doing anything to keep her mind off the upcoming event.

The earl had spared no expense on her wedding, and she knew that just beyond the doors, past the mountains of flowers that lined the aisle, her future husband, a man she could not see a future with, was waiting to make her his for all her life.

It seemed only as if it was last night that she was at her first ball, and here she stood, waiting to be married. Many months had passed since the first night she met Richard, and not one day since had passed that she had not thought of him and how he made her feel.

Sighing silently under her breath, she determined she was as ready as she was ever going to be. She took her place in front of the doors to the sanctuary. Pulling herself up straight, Margaret lifted her chin high. She was going to get through this.

Sarah came and handed her the bouquet of pink peonies,

giving her a reassuring smile. "It will be all right, my lady. You will see."

She started to form a rebuttal but decided to refrain, opting to say nothing instead. She was tired of fighting to convey her feelings. Besides, she knew her feelings did not matter.

If I just keep breathing one breath at a time and think of nothing else, I will get through this, she thought, trying not to let the panic set in.

Who was she trying to fool? She could not stay here and go through with this wedding! She was getting as far away as she could.

Margaret picked up the multiple layers of her dress, twirled around, and bolted quickly towards the front doors, pushing past a startled Sarah. She darted through the doors and into the bright spring light.

She glanced left, then right, then rapidly flew down the stairs. Turning to the right, she went around a corner, putting her back against the wall of the chapel and leaning her head against it.

Closing her eyes tightly, she sighed, shaking her head back and forth. What was she doing running away like that? This was not going to solve anything. At best, it would delay things a few minutes. But more than likely, it was only going to make the situation worse and create a scandal for the gossips to talk about.

"What are *you* doing out here?"

Her eyes flew open and head snapped to the side. She gasped in surprise. It was Richard!

She put her hand over her mouth without thinking and then forced herself to put it down slowly.

Margaret looked at the love of her life for several minutes, taking in his appearance. He did not look very well. In fact, he looked as if he had not slept since their last encounter at her home. His eyes were red and his hair was tousled. It hurt her to see him this way.

After several moments of silence, Margaret replied, "I could ask you the same. Why are you here? I thought you would be as far away from this place as possible."

He smiled grimly. "The thought had crossed my mind, but I decided to wait outside on the off chance that perhaps you would think twice about marrying him. I had hoped I would see you before you went through with this."

"Why?" she asked with puzzlement in her voice, and then added in defeat, "It is hopeless."

"You are wrong."

She licked her lips subconsciously and replied, "There is nothing I can do. My father has told me how it will be and nothing will change that." She blurted out with despair, "I... I cannot go through with it! I do not love him!"

"You have no choice now, unless...."

Hope flooded her as she ran up to him, grabbing his arm with both hands. "Unless what? Tell me. Whatever it is, I will do it."

"Unless... you run away with me." He gathered her into

his arms, whispering in a pleadingly urgent voice, "We can elope and spend our honeymoon abroad, and when things have settled down here, we can return as husband and wife."

Stepping back quickly, as if his mere words had physically slapped her, she stated, "I cannot do that! What of my father... Henry... my honor? It would be a huge scandal, and I cannot do that to them. It would kill my father and make Henry the laughingstock of England." She turned her back to him and whispered, "I am sorry I cannot do what you ask of me."

"But Margaret, you will never be happy with him. You know this, as do I."

"It is true. I know I will never feel for him the way I feel for you, but I am duty bound." She swallowed the lump that was forming in her throat as she clenched her eyes tightly shut. "I am sorry but this must be the last time that I speak with you." Margaret reopened her eyes, adding, "Please, this is my final request of you. Let me be, move on, and I will try to do the same."

He grabbed her arm and pulled her around to face him. "What of me? What of us? Does that not matter? Why can you not think of me or yourself before your duty?"

She averted her eyes. "My duty to my family comes first. I cannot disobey my father." She looked up to meet his eyes. "I want to be with you, but I know now it will never be."

Putting her hand on his arm, she pleaded with him, "Please, find someone else. Move on with your life... for I am lost to you. Forget me and let me go."

She started to turn away when he reached out to grab her, pulling her into his arms and whispering, "I will not. This will not end here. I swear it upon everything I hold dear. One day you will be mine, no matter what it takes."

And with that he leaned down and seared her with a kiss that pushed everything else out of her mind. She clung to him like a life preserver in the middle of a storm, engraining the feel of his lips and hands on her—knowing that once she left him this time, there would be no honorable way back into his arms.

After a few moments, he pulled away and looked down into her eyes, saying, "I will not let you go. Do you hear me? Never."

Margaret's desire for him took over and she kissed him. She dug her fingers into his hair, holding on, knowing that this would be the last kiss they would ever share. As she surrendered to his touch, he deepened the kiss and she wrapped her arms around his neck.

Pushing her against the wall, he kissed her face, ear, and throat, then worked his way back up. She kissed him back with more fervor, clinging to him, not wanting to let go.

He whispered in her ear, "My God, help me. I cannot let you go."

Her heart beat fiercely and her head was spinning out of control. She knew that if she did not stop this now, she would end up on a boat with Richard.

She turned her head to the side and, with a breathlessly ragged voice, said, "Stop! We must stop... this."

Ending his movements abruptly, he lingered only for moment, and then backed away from her. He stared at her without saying a word, waiting for her to make the next move.

She swallowed, trying to force the sudden dryness in her mouth away. "I have to go. I should have never come out here in the first place."

"But you did. Can you truly tell me that you can forget this?" he said as he leaned forward and brushed her lips with his own.

Shaking her head, she replied in a distraught whisper, "No, I cannot forget that or what I feel for you."

Sliding past him, she freed herself from his embrace and started to walk away, but then turned back around for an instant. "But I can push it away and not think about it. For my own sanity, that is what I must do. I beg you to do the same."

"This does not end here!"

Shaking her head in despair, she lamented, "I must go in now. They are waiting on me. I am sorry that it is ending this way."

She turned away from Richard and ran back the way she came.

CHAPTER 9

When Margaret entered the church, Sarah ran up to her. "Are you all right, my lady? Do you need anything?"

"I just need a moment, Sarah. All the excitement has made me a little faint. That is why I had to step outside to get some fresh air."

Sarah looked at her skeptically but said nothing. The earl came from one of the side doors and approached Margaret. "Are you ready, daughter?"

She wanted to scream, *No! I will never be ready for this!* But she knew creating a scene would get her nowhere and only infuriate her father. Instead, she said, "As I ever will be, Father."

Choosing to ignore Margaret's ambiguous response, the earl took her by the arm and guided her to the chapel doors.

He turned to her and said, "I love you, daughter, very much. You look so lovely today. I wish your mother and brother could have been here to share this with us."

"That would have been wonderful," Margaret said with a hint of melancholy in her voice.

He kissed her cheek and then pulled her veil down over her face.

Margaret took in a deep breath and leaned into her father, relying on his strength to get her through this.

The doors opened and she heard the string quartet playing the wedding march. As everyone stood, she realized all the pews were full to capacity. All eyes were on her.

Slowly, they walked down the aisle and she forced herself to look at Henry. Surprisingly, he seemed happy, and she had to admit he did look handsome in his black wedding suit.

Standing next to Henry was Reverend Portman, and as they approached the end of the aisle, the older gentleman gave her a sympathetic smile.

The earl handed Margaret over to Henry and then sat in the front row.

Henry took Margaret's hand and placed it on his arm. "You look beautiful, Margaret." Then they turned to face the reverend.

"Family and honored guests, we are gathered here today for the union of Lady Margaret Wellesley, daughter of the Earl of Renwick, and Lord Henry Wiltshire, the Viscount Rolantry. This day has been eagerly awaited as the happy couple has been betrothed for most of their lives. They have grown up together and have chosen today to make official their commitment to one another."

Margaret felt herself starting to shake, her knees buckling under the pressure. She made herself concentrate on getting through this without fainting. Her stomach was in knots and she could hardly breathe, but she was not going to make things worse by fainting.

"Do you, Lord Henry, take Lady Margaret to be your wedded wife, until death does part you?"

"I do."

"And do you, Lady Margaret, take Lord Henry to be your wedded husband, until death does part you?

Swallowing the lump in her throat, she forced out "I do."

"Now it is time for the exchange of rings, a symbol of your commitment to one another."

The couple placed the rings on each other's fingers, and then the reverend said, "By the power vested in me by God, I know pronounce Lord Henry and Lady Margaret husband and wife."

It was done. She was married to Henry, and she now had to live the rest of her life with that fact. It almost felt like she was in a daze and had just been going through the motions.

Everyone was clapping and she heard the reverend say, "You may seal the covenant with a kiss."

Henry leaned over and placed a gentle kiss upon her lips.

Margaret felt nothing. Defeated, she allowed Henry to escort her down the aisle and out of the church.

On the ride to Brookehaven, Margaret tried to come to terms with the situation, but she was unable to really wrap her mind around the fact that she was now wedded to Henry and she would never be with Richard.

As the carriage approached Brookehaven, she sat across from Henry in silence, dumbfounded because she felt so numb. With her head bent and her eyes focused on her hands in her lap, she could not think of anything but her despair.

She did not want to think about what was going to take place that night. Consummating their marriage vows frightened her. The mere thought of Henry touching her, kissing her like Richard had, made her want to jump out of the carriage while it was moving. Anything would be better than what was ahead of her.

Her biggest fear of all was that Henry was still mad at her about what had happened. If he was, he could take it out on her, and it was perfectly acceptable for a man to force his wife in the marriage bed or to beat her if she did not comply with his wishes. Not that she could see him doing anything like that, but the slight chance that he could and might really terrified her.

But perhaps, with all the festivities, Henry would be exceedingly tired and he would not want to be with her tonight. But of course, there was always tomorrow night and the night after that and the night after that....

She placed her face in her hands and shook her head from side to side. What was she going to do? There was no way out. She was caged by the very prison her father had configured.

Henry looked at her with puzzled eyes. "I know that our marriage has not taken place in the best of circumstances, but we *can* make the best of it. We are going to be together a long time, and I would like it to be a pleasant marriage. I would appreciate it if you would help me."

She glanced up at him and smiled grimly. "I will try."

"Margaret, it is time for us to go in for the celebration. I know that you do not want to, and quite frankly, neither do I, under the circumstances, but it is our obligation to our guests to do so and so we must."

After a few moments, they pulled up in front of the entrance to Brookehaven and the footman came around and opened the carriage door. With that, Henry took her hand and tucked it in the crook of his arm. Then he led her down the steps of the carriage and through the front door of her new home.

On the other side, two of Henry's female servants awaited their arrival to remove their cloaks and to help Margaret bustle her wedding dress for the upcoming festivities.

As the couple made their way into the ballroom, everyone she had ever known growing up was there. Her family and friends were all present, gathered together to congratulate them, not knowing what a sham the whole marriage truly was. She heard a big roar as they walked in and a bunch of shouts of congratulations and best wishes. Only a few seconds past before they were separated and each was pulled in opposite directions.

Baroness Wollingleer emerged from the crowd of women and pressed against Margaret, grabbing Margaret's arm and ushering her towards the ballroom, saying, "My dear, little Margaret, you finally got Henry to the altar, which is a very good thing too, since I hear that Lady Esther had her eyes on my godson. But we were all hoping it would be you, of course, my dear."

"I am sure you were, Lady Helen, but as you know this wedding took place actually earlier than everyone thought it would."

Giving one of her inordinate smiles, she replied, "Yes, well, our Henry did not want to lose you with the duke pursuing you and all. I mean, a duke! Who would have thought that our little Margaret would catch the eye of one so high?" She patted the younger girl's hand and continued, "Of course, in my day, I would have caught his eye as well. But looks fade, my dear, and soon you will see that." She glanced down at Margaret's figure meaningfully. "But of course, you made the wise decision." She leaned in towards Margaret, as if she were revealing a secret. "Moreover, I heard that the duke sought after you only in retaliation towards Henry. That, and your—" She paused, looking for the right word and adding the dramatic tension she loved to infuse into her conversations. "—unusual beauty, were the only reasons he threw in his suit for you at all."

She looked around and then turned back to Margaret, expecting to stir up some gossip. "So, my dear, we do seem to be missing the presence of His Grace. Where is the duke, by the by?"

Margaret was not in the mood for this. She stopped walking and turned to face the older woman, stripping off her pretenses and presenting the old bat with a glare. "How should I know, Lady Helen? I have been quite busy today with my wedding and have not been able to keep track of anyone else's schedule," she said tartly.

The Baroness cackled and replied, "Come, come, girl. This is between you and me. We both know you married Henry for convenience and, more pointedly, to please your father and fulfill a pact that he made with my beloved Henry's father. We both know that the ton does not frown upon discreet, shall we say, 'rendezvous' between the opposite sexes."

Narrowing her eyes, she frowned. "Lady Helen, think whatever you would like, but I am and will be faithful to my husband. I do not like what you are insinuating. Furthermore, I would advise you to let the whole subject alone. For the future, know that I will not be your source of gossip." Then, with a terse curtsy, she added in a clipped tone as she turned away, "Good eve, Lady Helen."

With that, Margaret abruptly departed towards the ballroom, leaving the flabbergasted baroness alone.

Oh, how she hated that... that bandy of a woman! She

had known right from the start that Lady Helen had been fishing about the love triangle between herself, Henry, and the duke. Margaret sure was not going to help that woman get any information about it. That was the last thing that needed to happen.

She despised these obligations. She hated people staring at her and picking her to pieces, as she well knew they did. And most of all, she hated Lady Helen and her circle of gossips that loved finding out everyone's dirty secrets so they could hold them over them, then use them against the person when he or she least expected it.

No one was dancing and she wondered why. Then she remembered that it was customary to wait for the bride and groom to start the ball with the first dance. Oh, how she hated traditions. If she were Queen of England, she would do away with them altogether. But then, that was wishful thinking

Tightening her lips, she tapped her fan on her hip as she listened to the music playing.

"You look sullen." She turned and glanced up at Henry.

"You know how I hate these functions and being the center of attention."

"Well, that is easy enough to fix. I will be the center of attention and you can come along in tow."

She attempted a smile. He always did have a way of making difficult situations seem easier. "I guess since you put it that way, I may not mind as much."

He took her hand once more, but instead of placing it on his arm, he took it in his own hand and pulled her along to the dance floor.

"I may not have had the privilege of your first dance at your first ball, but I will have the honor of your first dance at our wedding celebration."

He bowed before her gracefully, and after a moment's hesitation, Margaret curtsied in return.

"My lord."

"We are husband and wife now. Can you not call me by my given name?"

"As you wish… Henry."

He took her into his arms and they began to dance. Margaret focused on the steps to the waltz, and the couple danced for several moments without either of them saying a word.

Finally, Henry broke the silence by looking down at her and whispering softly, "This is not an ideal situation for either of us, but I think we can make it work."

Averting her eyes, she fell out of step for an instant.

"What is it, Margaret?"

She looked up and blurted out, "Why do you still want me? You know that I do not have the same feelings for you that you have for me. Why did you marry me?"

He touched her lightly on her cheek and tapped the tip of her nose playfully. "I have loved you all my life, Margaret. You are my best friend, my ideal woman, and now my wife all rolled into one." Pleading with his eyes, he added, "Please, try to help me make this work."

Continuing to evade meeting his eyes, she refused to give in to his demands. "I... I cannot, Henry. I do not think I am able to do what you want."

"You are, Margaret. You just do not want to, at least not yet. But you will because it is my intent to make you want me."

～

After several hours of dancing, eating, and drinking, the night was winding to a close.

"Can you believe that we are finally married?"

Shaking her head absently with her thoughts a million miles away, she contemplated what was coming soon.

She hated the fact that Henry practically owned her. In their society, husbands ruled over everything and women had no say whatsoever.

How was she going to be able to be intimate with him when she could not even think about letting him touch her, kiss her like Richard. The idea of doing what a husband and wife were expected to do on their wedding night, made her quake in her dancing slippers. There had to be a way around it.

"You are nervous. I realize this. But here is something you probably never thought to hear me say: I am as well. You see,

I want tonight to be perfect, yet I have this fear I will wake up and you being here with me will be a dream."

"It is all too real for me, I fear. I do not know what to do. I want to please you, but I fear that I will not."

He grinned at her. "Just you being my wife pleases me more than you will ever know. You were so beautiful when you walked down the aisle at the church. Despite everything, I could not wait to become your husband and start our new life together."

She forced a smile, trying to mask the guilt she felt over her indiscretion with Richard earlier in the day. "You think much too highly of me, Henry. Truly, I do not deserve such high favor. I think I will only make you unhappy as time goes on."

Opening his mouth to respond, he was halted when the earl appeared beside them.

"There you two are. I had wondered where you had gotten off to. I see that the two of you are talking—a good sign."

Margaret turned to face her father, waiting for him to continue.

"Well, the guests have all assembled downstairs to see you up to the bridal chambers. Are you ready?"

She looked over at Henry, who appeared as eager as a schoolboy at his first day of school.

Realizing that this was the perfect opportunity for her to avoid consummating their wedding, she prepared to claim that she was too tired and needed to sleep.

Henry would be unable to argue with the guests so close by.

She took back what she said about traditions. She did not hate them too much if they helped her in the long run, and by God, this one was going to help.

Hugging her father, she laughed. "All right, Father, if you are so anxious to see us upstairs, then by all means, we are ready. Are we not, Henry?"

Taken aback by her quick acceptance, he raised his eyebrows and replied, "Yes, by all means, let us make our way to the marriage bed."

He grabbed her hand and all the assembled guests made their way to the bridal chamber.

The guests surrounded them as they ascended the spiral staircase. The men were patting Henry on the back and the women were giving Margaret hugs. There was laughter, merriment, and lots of shouts of good luck as they reached their destination.

Baron Wollingleer opened the door and ushered everyone in. Several of the women took her into her dressing room and helped her disrobe while a few of the men helped Henry do the same. Then, after putting them in their nightclothes, the women brought her back to the sitting room and her father started to speak.

"On behalf of all the guests gathered here in your honor, we want to congratulate you and wish you both the best. May your marriage be filled with love, joy, and many children." He winked at his daughter. "Many, many children."

"We are counting on it, Henry," Margaret heard the Baroness Wollingleer shout above the other voices.

Another voice shouted, "Yes, Henry, do not let us down. Make us proud." She recognized the voice of Baron Wollingleer.

They were such an obnoxious couple. Leave it to them to make her blush with embarrassment.

The newly wedded couple was led into the bedroom. Husband and wife turned to face their guests and stood there looking like two odd pieces to a puzzle.

Slowly, the guests left, giving their final words of advice and congratulations, until finally they were left alone.

As soon as the door clicked shut behind the last guest, Henry turned to Margaret with his face shining with anticipation. "So, this is it. I have waited for this moment for so long, I cannot believe that it is finally happening."

Margaret whirled away and started to make her way over to her private chambers, saying, "I am tired, Henry. Perhaps we can do this tomorrow night. I truly am quite exhausted, and I see no sense in having to do this tonight."

Henry rushed up behind her and pulled her around to face him. "I realize that you are tired, and so am I, but I promise you will not regret staying up a little longer."

He moved towards her, and she stepped back cautiously. He smiled and said, "Do not be afraid. Come here, my love. I want to hold you."

She studied him for a moment. She was quite sure he was

not going to hurt her, but she still feared what was coming nonetheless.

Despite her protesting mind, she stepped forward and into his arms. She stood stiff and still, afraid if she moved, her perfectly constructed control would collapse.

"It is all right. I promise that it will be all right. Here—" He caressed the side of her face. "—let me lead you in this." Henry reached down and gently removed the elaborate comb from Margaret's hair, allowing her curls to cascade around her.

Reluctantly, she let him take her by the hand and guide her over to the marriage bed. He laid her down upon it and joined her, and then ever-so-gently kissed her forehead, eyebrows, cheek, and eyelids.

Margaret went rigid in her husband's arms when he leaned down to kiss her mouth. The only man she had ever kissed intimately was Richard, and she had no idea what it would feel like to kiss someone else.

She opened her eyes in surprise. Shockingly, his kiss was not repulsive as she thought it was going to be. It did not evoke the surges of passion that Richard's kisses did, but it was not unpleasant. Still, she remained stiff, hoping Henry would give up his attempts.

He began to touch her in new places and kiss her in tender spots, provoking reactions in Margaret. Against her own will, she began to feel sensations that she could not explain. How was he able to cause her body to betray her this way? Troubled by the way she was responding to his touch, Margaret squirmed to get free.

"Oh no, my love, you are not getting away from me, or *this*," he said as he firmly kissed her lips once more.

And with that last declaration, Henry taught Margaret things that night she never knew she wanted to feel or could. He showed her the essence of true love, and Margaret's life would never be the same again.

CHAPTER 10

*E*xhausted from the previous night's activities, Margaret stretched out her body as she yawned. She opened her eyes to find Sarah entering the room.

Her father had asked if any of the family servants wished to switch households with Margaret. Sarah did not hesitate to accept. Henry welcomed any of her servants who wished to join them, telling Margaret he was willing to do anything to make her transition more agreeable.

"My lady, the viscount sent me up to check on you and to let you know that the afternoon meal will be served in an hour. He has requested, if you are obliged, that you join him for it."

Margaret focused her eyes and looked at her companion. Sarah had her eyes averted. She frowned at Sarah in puzzlement. Margaret wondered why her servant reacted with such awkwardness, but then she realized that underneath the sheet, she was completely naked. Blushing, she remembering the night before and quickly pulled the covers up around her.

After the embarrassment passed, Margaret found herself amused at the thought that she finally knew what it meant to be a woman. Ironically, it had been Henry who had taught her when she had been so sure that it would have been at the hands of Richard.

"Um, yes, tell my... husband that I will be down shortly after I get dressed. And please have a servant sent up to assist me."

"As you wish, my lady."

Sarah quickly made her way out of the room.

Margaret chuckled to herself. It was probably the last way that Sarah thought to find her: naked in Henry's bed. Well, she supposed life was full of surprises.

Jumping out of bed, she looked around for her night-gown, finding it discarded in a heap with Henry's night-clothes. With fast precision, she untangled the two sets of clothing and pulled her gown on, then slipped on her dressing robe.

She exited Henry's bedroom and went to her own new set of rooms. There, she quickly looked around and located the vanity. She walked over and sat down in front of the mirror, staring at herself for several long moments.

Some of the changes were obvious. Never in her whole life had she looked like she did now. Her hair was in disarray, her face still bright from the lovemaking, and she had a new shine in her eyes that had never been there before.

But there were more changes that were even subtler. She could not exactly explain it, but she could feel the difference. He had awakened something in her that had never been there before. She now knew what it felt like to be a *satiated* woman.

Looking down at the table, to find something to comb her hair, to her surprise, she found her own personal items there. Her father must have had her belongings brought over before the wedding.

She picked up her hairbrush and began to comb her hair. She did not want the servants to see her this way. After attempting to pull through the tangles, Margaret gave up and winced. It was no good. Her hair was going to give her away. She tried to shake it into place, but it was no use. She was just going to have to wait.

Then she added some powder to try and hide her new heightened color, but she only accomplished in making the red stand out even more against the rest of her white skin.

"I guess this is as good as it is going to get," she said to herself. She started to pick up the hairbrush to try again to tame her hair when she heard a door open. She glanced into the mirror to see who it was, but instead only heard soft whispering voices and several giggles, followed by laughter.

She turned to find two of her personal servants. When they realized their mistress was staring at them, they stopped whispering and quickly lined up at attention.

"Good morning, ma'am. We have come here to dress you for dinner."

"Thank you, girls."

"The viscount wanted us to inform you that your belongings were delivered yesterday and we placed them in your new chest of drawers. He also had several new dresses made for you as a wedding gift."

"I think my husband would appreciate seeing me wear one of the new dresses. Bring me a blue one." Blue was Henry's favorite color, and she wanted to make the effort to please him.

After Margaret was dressed, she left her chambers and headed towards the dining hall. Several servants passed by and politely addressed her. As she rounded a corner to head towards the staircase, she encountered a girl she had never seen before at Brookhaven.

Wearing a tailored green dress of superior quality, Margaret knew she was not one of the servants. Something about her eyes made her stop the girl by saying, "I would like to ask you a few questions."

The girl nodded and replied, "Of course, my lady. I wish for you to get to know me, as does Henry."

She was surprised to hear this girl address Henry so informally. Who was she and how did she get away with it?

As she examined her, Margaret realized she was not really so much a girl as a budding young woman. She looked to be about sixteen and was striking in appearance. Perhaps even the most gorgeous girl Margaret had ever seen.

Her long auburn hair shined and danced like fire around her face, and her petite frame, had graceful lines that were just starting to curve in all the right places. But her most striking feature were her entrancing brown eyes. It was the girl's eyes that intrigued her the most. They seemed somehow familiar. Was she related to any of her servants?

Along with her intoxicating beauty, she had an innocence about her. She was pretty, but Margaret's fascination with her went deeper.

She looked at the girl for several minutes, inspecting her without saying anything. The girl fidgeted under the scrutiny.

"What is your name, and why are you here?"

Curtsying with her eyes averted, she replied, "My name is Catherine, my lady, and I was on my way to introduce myself when you stopped me. Henry asked me to help you in any way I can."

"He did, did he? Well, why is it that you address my husband so informally?" she snapped.

The girl's eyes widened in alarm as she replied, "The truth be, my lady, Henry asked me to do so. He has allowed me to live here so that I can be close to him."

Margaret was taken aback by the bluntness of the little strumpet. She was telling her new mistress that she had an interest in her husband and was not even batting an eye. She pressed her lips together and clenched her hands at her side.

"You wanted to be *close* to him," she said with a forced even tone. "Well, I will take care of that." She turned away and was going to leave it alone, but her anger got the better of her. She turned back around and added, "How dare you address my husband in such a way! You are insufferable and need to be taught some manners."

The girl's lower lip began to tremble and she bit it. Margaret could see that she was trying to hold back tears, but the mortification and hurt that Margaret had just subjected her to won out and the tears forced their way out, cascading quickly down her cheeks. Sobbing, she turned and fled down the hall.

Margaret was not about to have dinner with Henry after this. She returned to her chambers and began to undress.

To think, all this time she thought that he really loved her. What a fool she was to have believed him.

Oh, how she was going to let Henry have it when she saw him. She was so angry that she could have screamed. He had only married her yesterday, and he continued to keep his mistress at the estate, *their* home. Not only that, but he had asked his mistress to be her new companion. That was downright cruel and mean. She would not have it.

Hearing someone enter the room, she turned around ready for a fight and found Henry.

He came to stand in front of her, and with a frighteningly soft voice, he said, "You made Catherine cry, and I *will not* tolerate it."

Shaking with fury, she blasted, "*You* will not tolerate *me* making that little trollop cry? How dare you come in here and try to make *me* feel I am in the wrong!" She glared at him with bitterness. "You have put me in an exceedingly humiliating and embarrassing situation and you are telling me that I am to blame? I cannot believe that you can stand here and defend her to me."

He looked at her with anger in his eyes. "She has done nothing to deserve the way you treated her. She has not cried like that since her mother died, and now thanks to you, she has one more reason to think she is inferior."

"She is a prostitute, Henry. She may not look like one, but you keep her here so that 'she can be close to you,' and that makes her one!"

He grabbed her and shook her hard. "That little girl, that 'prostitute' as you call her"—he glared down into Margaret's eyes—"is my *sister!*"

Dumbfounded, Margaret stared up at him, then stammered out in disbelief, "But… but she cannot be. That is impossible. You are an only child."

"I have no legitimate brothers or sisters, that is true, but Catherine is my half-sister. She was sired by my father and a servant."

"How? When? Why did you never tell me?" Margaret asked in confusion.

"I never told you because I did not know myself until recently. A few months back, I came across some of my father's papers. Amongst them was a couple of small painted portraits of Catherine as well as a couple of documents regarding her boarding school. At the time, I thought it was a bit odd, but my father had always been a little peculiar.

"It was not until I met Catherine a few days ago that I found out she was his illegitimate daughter. You see, my father had secretly sent her away for schooling. She only got back a week ago because her mother passed away and the funding my father had set up for her stopped. She came back to tell me who she was and to see if I would continue to support her."

He continued to hold Margaret, but his hands and arms were in a relaxed grip.

"As far as I know, Catherine is the only illegitimate child he has sired. I offered to send her back to boarding school, but she decided she wanted to stay here instead. I told the servants that Catherine is a distant relative staying with me indefinitely to keep the gossip from traveling between the estates.

"I plan to take care of her and provide for her just as if she were my full sister. I wish that she really were, so that she could have all the privileges I do."

Margaret felt like such an idiot. She had misjudged and ripped apart a little girl who was only trying to please her brother's wife because she loved him. It did not matter that she misunderstood their relationship; the fact was that she overreacted without knowing all the information. She had a horrible habit of jumping to the wrong conclusions.

Averting her eyes, she said to his chest, "I am sorry, Henry. Truly, I am. I did not know she was your sister... but I also know that it is not an excuse. I hope you can find it in your heart to forgive me, and I will apologize to Catherine."

Placing his hand under her chin and lifting her head, he said, "Look at me, love."

Obediently, she lifted her eyes to his and saw that the anger had dissipated.

"I am very protective over my little sister. She is all the family I have in the world—besides my godparents—and you, now. But I also am flattered that you got jealous enough to react the way you did. I did not even think that you would care if I took a mistress."

She glared at him with mischief in her eyes. "You better not even think about that, sir." She pulled back to playfully hit him, but he caught her arm before she could land the punch.

"Not that I was going to take a mistress, mind you. Come to think of it, I have never even had one." Lovingly, he tapped her nose and said with all seriousness, "You should know by now that you are the *only* one for me." Then, breaking the somber mood, he laughed while running his fingers through his hair. "It is you that I, on the other hand, need to watch out for. I need to make sure you are not making a cuckold out of me."

With mock anger, she lunged at him and yelled, "You... you cretin! I will have you know that I plan to be faithful to you even if it kills me. And you had better be just as loyal."

"You have my word, my love," he said before leaning down and kissing her lips lightly. "I will never betray you."

"Good. I would have had to beat it out of you if you did."

"You? Beat me?" he said in an incredulous tone.

She nodded with seriousness. "I am an excellent fighter, Henry. I would advise you to remember that."

He smiled and baited her, "Would you like to demonstrate your techniques, my lady, on how you plan to take me down?"

She blushed as she realized the full implications of his meaning. She shrugged and replied, "If you wish."

And with that she ran at him, but instead of getting her shot in, he lifted her up into his arms. He twirled around and around until both of them were laughing with dizziness.

"See how easy I am to defeat, my sweet? I surrender, and you did not even have to throw a single punch."

She looked up at him and asked, "Where are you taking me?"

"I am taking you to someplace where you can show me your techniques, which you claim to be so good at."

Laughing, she replied, "Well, if you insist."

"Oh, I do." And with that, he carried her into her bedchamber.

CHAPTER 11

*L*ooking at the girl, who was again biting her lower lip, Margaret realized why Catherine's eyes had looked so familiar. They were like a twin set to Henry's. "Catherine, I misunderstood the relationship between you and your brother. You see, he never told me that he had a sister. Of course, I should have guessed with those eyes. Only the Rolantry family members have them."

Margaret smiled at the girl who was staring at her with both fear and awe mixed on her face. "What I suppose I am trying to say is that I am sorry. My temper seems to have gotten the better of me, as usual. You see, I continuously jump to the wrong conclusions. I hope that you will accept my apology. I want us to be like sisters, if that is possible."

Catherine stared at her for a moment and then blinked, replying softly, "I would like that too, my lady."

She shrugged off the formality. "Please, call me Margaret. We are family now."

"As you wish… Margaret."

Gently taking her sister-in-law's arm, Margaret hooked her own through it, keeping Catherine firmly at her side as she began to walk. "Now, I would greatly appreciate it if you would help me with the running of things around here. I am sure that boarding school prepared you for such an endeavor and your help would be immeasurably valuable, if you will agree to it."

Catherine stared at her pointedly. "My lady—" Margaret raised an eyebrow at her, and Catherine quickly corrected herself. "I mean, Margaret." The girl bit her lower lip and continued, "I know that you are trying to be kind to me, but I know that you were taught, since you were just a little girl, how to run a house, and you have been running your father's estate since you were ten."

Margaret eyes rounded in surprise and she laughed with amusement. "I see that you have caught me telling a fib. I did not expect you to have studied your brother's intended wife so closely." She stopped walking and turned to Catherine, smiling at the girl. "You must be very protective of him."

Catherine nodded and replied, "Yes, he is the only family I have."

"I am glad that you love him so. If anyone deserves to be loved so much, it is my husband. Now, what is it exactly that your brother wanted you to do for me?"

"I assume, my lad—Margaret, that he wanted me to be your companion."

"I already have one, a very good one at that, and I cannot very well have two."

She saw Catherine's shoulders visibly fall and her lower lip tremble. The girl was on the verge of tears again and barely holding them back. She quickly finished her statement. "What I mean, Catherine, is that I already have a companion and I would much rather have you as a friend." She gently took the girl's chin in her hand and lifted so Catherine's eyes met her own. "What I am proposing is that you no longer consider yourself an outsider here but what you truly are: part of the family. Take your place at your brother's side."

The girl's eyes grew round as she shook her head vehemently in denial. "I cannot do that. One does not assume a position above their place. I am a servant's daughter, my lady, and I know and accept that I will spend the rest of my life loving my brother from afar."

"Listen to me, Catherine. Birth does not make the person. I have seen people who are peasants and illegitimate who are nobler than any titled person has ever been. Frankly, who your mother was does not matter. What *does* matter is that if your brother could, he would claim you as his legitimate sister. We can make it happen, and no one will ever know the difference."

Worried that someone might be aware of Catherine's true

parentage, Margaret asked, "Did your mother ever mention you to any of the other servants?"

"No, to hide me from the viscountess, my mother lied to everyone and said that I had died when I was two. I lived abroad with a governess until I was old enough to be sent to boarding school. When I came back after my mother's sudden death, I went directly to Henry. He advised me not to say anything to anyone about who I was."

"The fact that you lived your whole life away from here is to our advantage. You already have all the basics down. It seems that the viscount made sure that you had an education and proper training. I will finish it, prepare you, and then introduce you into society as our sister. You will have a title, wealth, and will be the envy of the entire ton. No one will doubt it with our backing, and there will be no one who can dispute it, especially since Henry never told the servants here at Brookehaven anything about you except that you are a distant relative. We can simply explain that away by telling everyone we wanted to allow you to familiarize yourself before bombarding you with visitors and suitors."

Getting into the whole idea, Margaret continued, "We will explain that your boarding school was overseas and that you have come home to marry and start your own family."

Catherine stopped walking and bit her lip. She stared at Margaret for a moment then yelped out, "Me? You want me to be introduced as your sister-in-law?"

Margaret raised an eyebrow and replied, "Of course you. Whom else would I be talking about?"

"I cannot, Margaret. It is a lie and it is wrong."

"But Catherine, it is not wrong because it is your right to claim your brother as your family. You deserve to be a part of this family. Henry loves you and would be proud to stand by you in front of the entire world, as would I."

Pure anguish crossed the girl's face right before she turned away and put her back to Margaret. Catherine's shoulders drooped forward, and she said in a soft whisper, "Do you know how long I wished and waited for my father to claim me as his daughter? My mother told me repeatedly that it would never happen and to accept things the way they were, but I could not, because part of me could not help wishing for it nonetheless.

"I used to lie in bed every night at boarding school, praying that he would claim me and that I would know what it was like to have a father, to not be something he had to keep secret. I wanted so badly to be a part of the Rolantry family, but he died and it never happened. Then Henry found out about me, and I regained some of that hope. I thought that when he discovered the truth, he would find a way to claim me as his sister. But again, it did not happen." She turned back around and whispered in a choked voice, "You know what I came to realize?"

"What, Catherine?"

"I came to realize that it was never going to happen, and it would have to be enough to know that Henry loved me."

She walked past Margaret and headed for the side door. She stopped and then pivoted for a moment, adding, "I am a servant's daughter, my lady, and that is what I will always be. No introduction to society will ever change that."

"If I thought that you truly believed that, then I would let it be, but I know that you must desperately want to be a part of this family or you would have returned to your boarding school. You stayed around here in hopes of making an official bond with your brother, and I am going to make it my ambition to see that it happens."

CHAPTER 12

*P*leased with herself, for not only obtaining Catherine's forgiveness, but hopefully earning respect in Henry's eyes by helping his sister, Margaret chose to reward herself with a ride.

Expertly gripping the reigns to Charlie, Margaret allowed the horse to meander along one of the trails. She always thought more clearly when she was riding.

Catherine already had all the training needed in the areas of manners, knowing protocol and such, but Margaret needed to teach her how to take her place in society as a titled lady since she had never been to finishing school. This would be no easy feat. She would have to teach her how to act in any social setting, as well as how to dance, dress, and present herself as if she had always been part of the titled.

Unfortunately, it was quite a challenge to change the

mind of someone who considered themselves inferior. But Margaret was determined to do it, and she knew she could.

Deciding not to tell Henry of her plans had posed diffi cult, but Margaret knew once he saw the remarkable changes in his sister, he would not be able to say no to introducing her into society.

She congratulated herself on her cleverly crafted plan. Not only was she going to win Catherine over but she would also gain more of Henry's favor.

Margaret saw a grove of trees just up ahead and slowly brought Charlie to a halt. She dismounted and looked around. No one was in sight. Good. She quickly undid the top few buttons of her ivory blouse and walked over to a nearby patch of wild flowers. She picked a few and put them throughout her hair.

Grateful that she was able to get away by herself for a few moments, she had been surprised that Henry had said she could go. But then, he had been preoccupied with his business issues, so he really was not paying attention when he said it was all right. She had left as fast as she could so he could not change his mind.

Needing to sort out some of the feelings and thoughts that were racing through her mind about her own life, she contemplated how her life had changed. Margaret used to be so certain about what she wanted, but since Richard entered her life, everything had been turned upside down. The more time she spent married to Henry, the more she began to see her father's point and realize that Henry was a good husband. He was completely devoted to her, putting her above everything else in his life. But realizing this put her in turmoil, because how could she have thought so certainly that she would only love Richard for the rest of her life and now realize that she had feelings—real, true feelings—for Henry as well? Was she falling in love with Henry? She was not sure.

She was humming to herself lightly as she pondered her feelings when she heard something from behind. Quickly turning around, she found Richard standing a few yards behind her.

Gasping, first in surprise, then shock, she smiled awkwardly at the duke. "I did not expect to see you after the wedding," she said.

He looked at her a few moments without saying or doing anything. Then he circled her, stopping a few feet in front. "Indeed." He narrowed his eyes. "Something has changed in you, little one."

She did not say anything but continued to watch him.

"What are you doing out here alone?"

"I decided to go for a ride today."

Spitting out the words, Richard said, "You mean to tell me that your husband actually allowed you out of his sight?"

As he walked towards her, Margaret recognized the frustrated look on his face. The duke halted just within arm's length, reached out, and took a hold of her. "I know if you were my wife, I would never let you out of mine."

Richard looked even worse than he had on her wedding

day. It appeared as if he had not slept since that day. His face was drawn, his hair and clothes disheveled, and he smelt faintly of alcohol.

She averted her eyes and replied, "He was quite busy when I left. I do not think he even noticed I had gone."

He sighed and shook his head, saying sarcastically, "It is such a shame that he does not pay more attention to you." Richard brushed the side of her face with his hand as he whispered in a steely voice, "I have been waiting for you to leave his estate so I could talk to you alone."

"Why? What is it that you wish to discuss with me? I thought I made it perfectly clear where I stood the last time we spoke."

"What is it that I wish to discuss, you ask? Let me see… perhaps that I am going crazy and it is due to you." His frustration was audible. "I pace my study, hour after hour, trying to forget about you, but I cannot get you off my mind. Look what you have done to me." He wildly gestured at his appearance. "I know now that you have traded me in for another and no longer want me."

She shook her head in denial. "No, Richard, it is not like that at all. You have no idea what I have gone through since the wedding."

Uttering every word pointedly, slicing through her with the precision of a surgeon, he said, "You? What *you* have gone through? Do you know how I stay up all night every night since you left me standing there at the church to marry *him?* And when I do try to sleep from sheer exhaustion, I toss and turn, then scream with rage and pain at the thought of him touching you, taking you and branding you with his flesh! My servants think that I am going mad. Part of me thinks that they are right. It torments me, Margaret, the thought of him having what should be *mine*."

Trying to pull away because his hands were digging into her skin, she winced, saying, "Let me go. You are hurting me."

"No, you enchantress, I will not let you go. You have besotted me, and I cannot even function because of how you haunt my thoughts, my memories, my dreams. I want so badly to hold you again, to kiss you and feel you quiver beneath my touch. But he has you. My God, he has those rights, and I am left with nothing." He stared down into her eyes for a moment. "But I will taste you again, my sweet." Dipping down until she could feel his breath play across her face, he said, "Right now is as good a time as any."

She yanked free and said, with more force than before, "Let go. I mean it. I think you are bruising me."

Mockingly, he gave her a sardonic smile. "You used to like it when I held you close. Ah, but let me guess. You have had a change of heart and no longer love me. Instead, you are completely devoted to your new husband and now want nothing to do with me."

Her eyes rounded and she clamored in her own defense. "You are wrong, my lord. It is not as you say."

Laughing with scorn, he grabbed her roughly, pulling her

towards him again. "So, now it is 'my lord.' You cannot even call me by my given name."

He started to brush light kisses over her face and neck, but she was done letting him try to use her desires against her. She put up her hands and pushed hard against his chest.

Once free, she stated firmly, "I am sorry but this is, at an overwhelming rate, becoming a very compromising position for me."

Glaring at her, he railed, "So, you have discarded your love for me just like that. What a fickle girl you are, my dear."

She shook her head in rebuff. "That is not how it is, Richard. I do still love you!"

He once more pulled her back into his arms. "Then show me. Show me that you still love me."

And with that, he brutally forced his lips upon hers. At first, she accepted his kiss because part of her desperately wanted to feel him again, and she also felt obligated to prove her devotion to him. But the kiss felt more like a punishment than an indication of love. The more sensible part of her realized that it was a betrayal to both her husband and honor. She tried to pull away, but he was physically stronger.

In between breaths, she begged him, "Please... let me... go. I... cannot... do this!"

When her pleas did not dissuade the duke's harsh abusive behavior, she made an effort to turn her head to the side so that he could not reach her mouth anymore. But it was as if the more she squirmed, the further heightened his desire became and the more brutal he made the kiss.

Finally, she went limp and impassive, hoping that if she did not do anything he would let her go.

He continued to kiss her and was about to force her onto the ground when a voice interrupted, saying, "Witherton, I think it best if you release my wife and step away from her."

The duke slowly, as if he had nothing better to do, let her go and stepped back. With a bored voice, he said, "Hello, Rolantry. What brings you out this way? Checking up on your wife, are you?"

Coming out of the forest, Henry walked over to where they stood. He smiled with fake friendliness. "Why, I came to meet my wife, of course. I promised her that as soon as I was done with my work I would come join her for a dip in the lake. Thank you, Your Grace, for keeping my wife company, but she has an escort now and your 'services' are no longer needed."

Worried that Henry thought she planned to meet Richard here, she hoped he realized that it was all the duke's doing.

Witherton eyes grew wide in surprise, and then he glanced at Margaret with a quick look of disgust.

Henry looked at his wife, saying with forced levity, "I am sorry, my love, that I am late, but you know how my business matters sometimes take longer than I expect." He turned back to face the duke, smiled, and said, "Now, if you will excuse us, we do not have much time before we need to be back for our midday meal."

The duke bowed in mock respect and replied derisively,

"By all means, then, do not let me keep you waiting. Enjoy your dip. I hear that newly wedded couples often do."

With that he turned and walked over to his horse and, within moments, galloped out of sight.

Henry walked over to where Margaret was standing. He looked her up and down and then asked, "Well, are you all right?"

She nodded without answering, still rubbing her bruised arm, trying to forget how it felt to have the duke hurt her the way he had.

"What was he doing here with you, anyhow?"

She looked at him. "He said that he had been waiting for me to leave the grounds so that he could talk to me. He found me out here while I was picking wildflowers."

Glancing at the flowers that were in disarray in her hair, he stated, "I can see that." He plucked one from her hair and rubbed a petal between his fingers.

"I was about to go back to Brookehaven when he startled me from behind."

"Then perhaps you should not go riding by yourself again."

She was about to balk at the idea and argue but thought better of it. "Perhaps you are right," she replied instead. Then, as Margaret thought about the conversation that had passed between her husband and the duke, she quickly asked, "What was all that nonsense about us going for a swim in the lake? I did not even know there was a lake on your estate."

He smiled at her. "I was weeding out a weasel, my dear, if

you must know. And if you are curious about my lake, then I suggest you take me up on my offer and go swimming with me."

Margaret laughed, relieved that Henry was ready to move on and not allow the duke to ruin the progress they had made in their relationship. She replied, "All right, Henry, take me to your lake. But know I only come due to the fact that my curiosity has gotten the better of me."

"You will not regret it."

CHAPTER 13

The lake was breathtaking. She had never seen a place as beautiful as this. It was crystal clear, surrounded by majestic weeping willow trees and beds of wildflowers in every color imaginable. She turned around to face her husband and smiled.

"It is magnificent, Henry! I cannot believe that you have never shown this to me before."

He shrugged. "I wanted to save it for when we married. I wanted the first time you saw it to be special because it is a special place for me. I have never taken anyone here until now. This is my place, and now it is ours."

Looking up into his eyes, she said, "I like that. *Our* place."

Margaret took off her shoes and stockings to dip her toes in the water. "It feels refreshing, Henry."

"I am pleased you think so. Now get out of those clothes so we can go for a dip."

Her eyes narrowed in disbelief. "You are serious? You really want to swim? Naked?" She shook her head. "I do not think so, Henry. I shall never swim naked in this lake, or in any other lake for that matter."

Henry smiled impishly. "Well, you have two options. Either you can willingly get out of your clothes or... I can throw you in. Then you will end up taking them off or drowning to death due to your modesty."

As she started to walk towards her horse, she said, "We had better be on our way so we can get back for the midday meal."

Grabbing her arm, he pulled her back. "I do not think so, my dear. You will swim with me one way or another."

Margaret smacked his hand away. "Whatever do you mean?"

Grinning with a chuckle, he said, "Simply that if you do not go in winningly, I will throw you in."

"You would not dare!"

He raised an eyebrow. "You think not, do you? I will have you know that I very well intend to carry out my threat." He quickly grabbed her around the waist.

She pulled free from his grasp and darted behind a tree, looking around as she tried to plan an escape route.

"These games are only delaying the inevitable. I will win, my lovely Margaret. I am bigger, faster, and much, *much* more determined than you."

"Henry, imagine what the servants will think if I come home in wet clothes. They will speculate about what occurred between us… and you know how I *despise* servants gossiping about me."

"Well, if you do it my way, then your hair can dry und your clothes will not get wet. But if you are stubborn, like you usually are, then I guess the servants will just have to wonder…."

Stepping out from behind the tree, she glanced at where her horse stood and pressed her lips together tightly. It was only a few feet. She could make it if she sprinted right now.

But, as if Henry read her mind, he stepped in front of her escape route. "Oh, no you do not. You are not getting away that easily."

She tried to get around him. "This is insane, Henry. It is getting late and we should be heading back."

He grabbed her and asked, "Well, which is it going to be? Are you going to cooperate, or am I going to have to throw you in?"

"You can swim if you like, but I am going home." She tried to push past him, but before she knew what was happening, he swung her up and over his shoulder as she kicked and pounded on his back. "Let me down, Henry! This is absurd. Oh, you… you beast. Let me down this instant." She was so intent on making him let her go that she barely recognized that, all of a sudden, she was in midair. Then she was submerged in water and sinking towards the bottom of the lake.

She kicked up to get some air as her blouse, thick pants, and underclothes began to bunch up on her. Realizing she could not swim freely with them on, she removed them hurriedly and held them in one hand as she treaded water.

Margaret glanced up at the shoreline to find Henry standing on the banks fully naked in the sunlight.

Ignoring the rush of desire that flooded her, she yelled at him, "What are you doing just standing there? I could have drowned, you know. And you were not even going to help me."

Looking amused, he laughed. "I was quite sure you could manage to take care of yourself and rectify the situation. And look, you did."

With that, he jumped into the water and joined her. "You see I told you, either way, you were going to be swimming naked with me." He splashed some water at her and finished, "Now I suppose you will just have to live with the servants' gossip."

He grabbed her wet clothes from her hands and threw them onto the bank next to her stockings and shoes.

"Oh, you." She lunged at him, but he quickly darted away.

"You should know better than to let your temper fly with me." And with that, he grabbed her and pulled her close. "I love you, Margaret. Tell me you love me too."

She tried to pull away but stopped struggling when she realized she could not get free. Then she replied, "You are my best friend, Henry. I have always loved you."

"That is not what I meant and you know it. I want you to tell me you are in love with me."

"I cannot. Please, let *this* be enough."

He stared at her with seriousness and said, "Then I guess I will just have to do a little more convincing."

Henry leaned across the water and took possession of her mouth. Margaret was not really prepared for the onslaught of his kiss. It was unlike any of the other kisses they had ever shared before. It was much more demanding and possessive, but it also evoked stronger, more potent emotions in her that did exactly what he said they would. By the time he was ending the kiss, she realized that she did not mind the circumstances at all. She leaned into her husband as he pulled her more fully against him.

"There are a thousand new and exciting things that I wish to show you, Margaret. Making love in water is only one of them."

As they lay on a bed of wildflowers and moss, tired and blissful from their lovemaking, Margaret thought of how everything was shifting in her life.

A few days ago, she never would have believed that she could have been happy with anyone but Richard. And here she was, lying next to Henry and as content as could be. Truth be told, she was enormously satisfied and supremely pleased.

She had a husband, a new sister, a beautiful manor, and all the money any one person could ever want. But yet there was a part of her that was empty, and it was *that* part that was keeping her from loving Henry fully.

Unable to shake the feeling something was missing, Margaret could not quite pinpoint what she lacked. She was quite certain that it was not Richard or anything else she could name, but she felt it nevertheless.

Leaning up on one elbow, she looked over at Henry. He was dozing off with a faint smile on his face. She was glad that she could make him happy. He deserved to be, but she could not help but feel a little selfish by wanting to be completely happy herself.

Margaret touched the side of his face with her hand and brushed away his thick blond hair.

She did not fully understand these new emotions that she was feeling for Henry. She knew they were wonderful, but they also scared her. She lost all control when she felt them, and Margaret hated being out of control.

So much of her life was decided for her that the one thing she had always been able to control were her feelings and how she showed them. But now, when Henry kissed her the way he had in the lake, she lost her perfectly constructed demeanor. She did not know how to handle it. Perhaps it was time that she let go and stopped trying to bottle it all up.

Sighing softly in contentment, she leaned forward and kissed Henry gently on the lips. As she pulled away, she saw one eye crack open and a smirk cross his face.

"So, my wife, I wake to find you ogling me while I sleep."

"Oh, you." She pinched him playfully. "You were awake the whole time."

He opened both eyes now and leaned up on his elbows. Jokingly, he replied, "So what if I was? I wanted to see what you would do while I slept defenseless in your arms. Would you stab me or drown me in the lake? I *had* to know."

She jumped up on her knees. "You are incorrigible! I cannot believe how you continuously dupe me into believing your fake innocence and lies."

"Yes, I know, I am such a *horrible* man. But you redeem me, my love. Will you not give a guilty man a pardon, my queen?"

Laughing, Margaret said, "You are atrocious!" Then she shrugged and said, "But I suppose I can give you leave if you do that thing you did earlier."

Raising an eyebrow, he leaned forward and grabbed her, then flipped her over onto her back. He began kissing her neck in a certain spot. "Do you mean this?" he said against her neck.

"Oh yes, that is part of it, but I mean the whole thing."

He leaned up slightly. "You want to again?"

She smiled coyly. "Only if you do, Henry."

Without another word, he bent down and continued the job he had started.

She could still feel the embarrassment from when they had

walked in through the side doors of their estate. She had tried to be discreet and get to her rooms before any of the servants saw them, but luck was not on her side.

Instead, Motty and Francisca were headed down the same hall they entered. The girls looked at them, took in Margaret's wet clothes and the couple's messy appearance, and hurried past them. She could still hear their giggles as they echoed down the hall.

When they reached their chambers, she turned around to confront him. Pointing a finger at him, she said, "See, I told you that the servants were going to find out. And just wait, soon it will spread throughout Brookehaven, and probably within the day throughout the county."

He frowned. "We are man and wife. What should it matter if people know what we do?"

"It matters because what we do behind closed doors is one thing, but what others know about our private life is quite another. I do not want anyone to know about what we do or where we do it."

A look of puzzlement crossed his face for a moment but was quickly replaced by anger. "Why? Is it because you fear that your precious duke will find out?"

Hurt flashed through her but was quickly replaced by her own rising anger. "No, it has nothing to do with him. To be perfectly honest, I do not even know if I have feelings for him anymore."

"I say, then why were you kissing him back when I came upon you in the clearing?"

She had hoped Henry had not seen her reaction to Richard. Margaret still felt physical attraction to Richard, but something changed out in the grove earlier. When he grabbed her and hurt her the way he had, she realized she really did not know the man. Was it possible that she had only been infatuated with the duke and had mistaken it for love? As she continued to get to know the duke, she realized she did not like the dark side that manifested when he did not get his way.

"I cannot explain what happened out there, Henry, but this I know: I will never hurt or betray you. You, your home, and your family are my life now. Nothing else matters, and I intend to do whatever it takes to make our life together happy."

He looked at her for several minutes before walking over to the window and looking out. His voice was quiet when he said, "I want to believe you, Margaret, I really do. But part of me insists that you still love him and it is only a matter of time before you give in to your desires."

She strode over to him and rested her hand on the back of his shoulder. "You are wrong. I could never do that because my honor is stronger than any desire or feelings I might have."

Pulling away slightly, he shook his head. "You just do not get it, do you? The fact is that I am jealous of him. I want those feelings, your desires, for me and me alone. I do not want you to just submit to me and be passive in our love-making. I want you to want me and need me. I want you to cry out my name, saying that you love me. And what disturbs me the most is one day I fear you will do those very things for *him*."

She did not know what to say. If she argued with him, it would just make her seem guilty, but if she did not argue, then it would seem as if it were true.

Without thinking, she pulled him around to face her. Placing a hand on each of his shoulders, she leaned up on her tiptoes and placed a sincere kiss upon his lips. It was the only thing she could think of that might express what she was trying to convey.

He stood there idly.

Not getting a response, she became more passionate, making the kiss more demanding. She felt him holding back, so she deepened the kiss and enfolded her arms around his neck, pulling him close.

That move was his undoing. Pulling her into his arms, he kissed her back with fervor.

He wrapped an arm around her waist while he tugged on the wet blouse that clung to her. Impatiently, he jerked on the back and yanked it off with one stroke.

Gruffly, he mumbled, "I will buy you a new one, my love. Ten outfits if you want them." He began to work on removing her riding pants as he continued to kiss her. Once he had divested her of her clothes, he led her to their bedroom, whispering, "You win this round, my dear. But then, you always do."

CHAPTER 14

*E*verything was going well with Catherine's training. Margaret could not wait to see the look on Henry's face when she presented his sister to him as a lady.

The two of them stood in the parlor where Margaret had been drilling Catherine for days about etiquette, proper protocol, and various other social aspects she needed to know if she wanted to pass as a noblewoman.

"All right, Catherine, now make sure that when you see someone of lower class you make them come to you. Also, you should never curtsy to anyone who is lower than you. Let them make the first move."

Standing still as Margaret circled her, Catherine maintained proper demeanor. Stopping at the young girl's side, Margaret continued, "I think that you are almost ready. All we have left is a few more proper dining and etiquette lessons as well as equestrian training. Then we will be finished."

Catherine cringed. "Finished? But we only began a few days ago."

Margaret faced the girl and said, "Yes, but you knew most everything a lady needs to already. I only had to refine a few things and teach you a couple of others. That was easy enough since you are such a quick learner. Once you know how to ride a horse like a lady, as you will need to know how to do for fox hunts, you will be able to keep up with the ton without any problems."

The girl took a step back, stumbling slightly. "Ride? Did you say ride a horse?" She bit her lower lip, a habit that Margaret was trying to break her of. "Must I?"

"Do not bite your lower lip, Catherine. And yes, riding is a requirement as part of the titled." Then a realization struck. "Do you not know *how* to ride a horse?"

"At boarding school, there was never a need for me to know how to ride." She looked away for a moment and then continued with an edge of fear in her voice. "I am also petrified of horses, Margaret. They terrify me."

Margaret looked at her sister-in-law for a moment and asked, "Is there a reason why you are afraid of horses?"

"Yes, but I do not wish to talk about it."

"I think you must in order to get past it. I think it will be the only way that we will be able to finish your training."

Catherine stood still for several seconds. Then her voice lost all emotion as she said, "Perhaps I was right after all when I said that I would always be a servant. I just do not think that I am meant to be part of the nobility. Now if you will excuse me, my lady, I need to be going about my duties."

She turned and started to walk away when Margaret stopped her. "Wait! You do belong. I can help you get past this fear of yours, but first, I must understand it." She reached out and touched Catherine's arm. "Please, let me help you."

Turning back around, Catherine stared over Margaret's shoulder as if she were battling with a ghost. "I was five when it happened. I had been playing hide-and-seek with Cecilia, my dearest friend. She was a daughter of one of the servants who worked for us while I lived abroad with my governess. I was searching for Cecilia in the stables, even though I knew that we were not supposed to be in there, when I heard this noise, like whimpering. I followed it to see what it was, thinking it was a lost baby kitten or something, but when I arrived at where it was coming from, I spotted Cecilia curled up in a ball in the corner of a stall. She had spooked a horse and it had reared up.

"I stood there, frozen with terror as I watched the horse's front legs come down and trample my friend. It must have already done so before because there was so much blood all over her, coating her hair, her face. I just stood there for several seconds, and when she did not move, I whispered, 'Cecilia?' as if calling her name would bring her back. But she continued to lie there, unmoving in a puddle of blood.

"That was when the impact of what had occurred hit me

and I ran screaming into the house. The governess asked what had happened, but I just kept screaming and screaming. She held me the whole night as I alternated between screams of terror and sobs of fear. For years after that incident, I had nightmares. Infrequently, I still do. I am *deathly* afraid of horses. I barely look at them and I break out in a sweat." Catherine's eyes refocused and she looked at Margaret. "Perhaps now you understand why the mere thought of riding them is beyond me."

"I do see where you are coming from, and I think I understand. My brother was... killed by sharks off the coast of France when I was ten. I did not believe he was dead at first, but once the truth set in, I was petrified of the ocean. I just knew that if I went into the water, sharks were going to kill me too. But after several trips to the sea and me refusing to go in the water, my father said it was time I face my fear. So I did. I made myself go in the water. It was probably one of the hardest things I have ever done. But I went out, and after that, it was like the ocean had no power over me anymore. I began to respect it and realize that we need the sea to survive, and I was able to swim without fear." Smiling, Margaret continued, "If you can learn to find respect for the thing you fear but not let it control you, then you will be able to let go of your fear."

Putting on a brave face, Catherine replied, "If you will stay with me through it, then I shall try, Margaret."

"Good! We will start tomorrow." She turned to Catherine and asked, "I will see you for dinner this evening, will I not?"

Catherine nodded. "I am going to go upstairs and take a bath beforehand, and perhaps take a small nap."

"A bath sounds heavenly. I think I will have one as well since I feel a bit tired."

Once upstairs, Margaret requested that a bath be drawn for her, and since the natural light was fading as night approached, the servants also lit several candles and placed them around the room. Once the servants had left, Margaret disrobed and slowly slipped into the porcelain tub.

The warm water felt magnificent, and she leaned back in the tub and began relaxing. She did not see Henry walk in as she hummed softly to herself and soaked in the water. When he came up behind her and rested his hands on her shoulders, she jumped and twisted around, then sighed with relief when she saw that it was him.

"You startled me, Henry. I was so wrapped up in my bath that I did not here you come in." Hoping to tempt him, she smiled and asked, "Would you like to join me? The servants brought in a tub big enough for two. It was assuming of them to do so, but then, I am not going to complain."

He began to massage her shoulders and back. "Perhaps in a moment, but right now, I want to indulge my wife."

Margaret moaned, loving the feel of his touch on her skin. "Oh Henry, that feels so exquisite." She looked up in his eyes and said pointedly, "You have incredible hands."

He raised an eyebrow. "You think so, do you? Well, let me see what else I can do with them."

Reaching down, he picked up the bar of soap, lathered it

in his hands, and then began to wash her hair. As she groaned even more, he chuckled.

"You like that, do you? Well, there is plenty more where that came from." He continued to wash her hair, massaging while deepening the strokes.

Margaret was fully aware of her own desire. The way he was washing her hair was evoking the most sensual emotions she had ever felt.

"Please, join me," she begged as she put one of her hands on top of his, tangling both of their hands in her hair. Demandingly, she pulled, beckoning him.

As he slowly removed his hands from her hair, he replied, "All right, if you insist."

"I do."

He came around to stand in front of her as he removed his clothing. She held in a breath while she took in his perfect male body and watched with anticipating eyes as he stepped into the water.

Leaning forward, he pulled her into his lap and gently pushed her hair over to one side of her neck. Then he began to kiss the other side.

"I am glad that you joined me, Henry."

"As am I, my love."

"Are you ready for this, Catherine?"

Catherine nodded and the stable boy helped her mount

the tamest horse Margaret could find.

Both women were dressed in freshly pressed riding outfits: Margaret wore a dark purple and black set and Catherine donned a green and tan outfit that Margaret let her borrow. Catherine's new clothes for her introduction into society were being made and would not be ready for several more days.

"Margaret," Catherine said in a shrill voice, "I do not think I can do this!"

After mounting her horse, Margaret came up next to Catherine. She took hold of the other horse's reins and murmured, "Whoa, whoa now. Settle down, boy."

She looked at Catherine, who was stiff as a board, and said, "Remember what we went over. You need to relax your body and loosen your grip. The horse can feel your tension, and that makes him nervous."

Margaret watched as Catherine made herself slowly calm down. Margaret was trying to be courageous for her sister-in-law's sake, but secretly she was afraid the girl's uneasiness would spook the horse. That was all they needed! If Catherine was already afraid of horses, being bucked off one would make it so that she never wanted to get on one again.

Wanting to keep the horse calm, Margaret continued to hold the reins firmly while gently stroking the horse's face as she whispered soothing words. Once she felt the horse was calm enough for Catherine to take over, she handed the reins back to her and said, "All right, now we are going to start out at a light trot. Remember to press in with your legs and guide him with your reins."

Catherine did as she was instructed while Margaret followed alongside.

"Good, you are doing well, Catherine. Now I need you to give the signal to bring him to a little faster trot. Remember how I taught you to do that."

Once again, Catherine carried out the instruction, and the horse started to trot faster.

"See, Catherine, you are doing fine and nothing bad is happening."

"It is not over yet, Margaret," she said in a small, shrill voice.

"But there is nothing to it once you get the basics down, and you have them." She paused for a moment, then continued, "I think it is time for us to call it a day. Remember how we went over cooling him down before stopping completely."

Catherine took the horse from a slow trot to a gait and finally to a stop.

"Thank you, Margaret, for making this possible. If not for you, I do not think that I would have ever gotten over this fear."

"Nonsense. It might have taken you a little while longer, but I have faith that you would have done fine on your own."

She laughed. "Perhaps you are right, but thank you nonetheless."

Margaret smiled in return. "You are very much welcome."

The two of them walked towards the house and chattered about the events of the morning. As they entered through the back door, Catherine sputtered in elation, "I am so happy that I was able to do this. I cannot believe that I actually followed through and was able to accomplish everything I did!"

"I know, I am so proud of you!"

Catherine hugged her sister-in-law, saying, "Thank you so much. I never thought I would be able to do that."

From around the corner, a voice asked, "Do what?" After a moment, Henry came into view and was gazing at them with curiosity.

Margaret replied evenly, making sure to hide her surprise at being overheard, "Catherine learned to ride a horse today."

He raised an eyebrow in puzzlement and asked, "You did not know how to before today?"

Catherine shook her head. "It was Margaret who encouraged me to try and helped me through it."

He looked at his wife with apparent respect and admiration. "Well done, my love. I am pleased that you have taken an interest in my sister."

Catherine's eyes opened wide as Henry called her his sister so openly. He had never done that before.

Patting his sister lightly on the back, Henry said with a grin, "Good job. Keep it up. Perhaps soon, all three of us can go on a ride and picnic."

Smiling, Catherine rushed forward, hugging her brother. "I would like that very much, Henry."

He looked over his sister and met Margaret's eyes. "How about you? Would you like that?"

"Very much, my husband."

"Then a picnic we shall have, and I think today is as good a day as any."

Both the women clapped their hands together in excitement and laughed.

"This will be so much fun!" Catherine squealed.

Margaret lovingly put her hand on Henry's arm and said, "I am so glad you decided to be spontaneous and give us this treat."

"My pleasure. I can think of nothing more charming than spending time with my two favorite ladies."

After having Cook put some food together for them in a picnic basket, Henry tasked a few of the other servants with gathering up the supplies they would need. Once they had all of their provisions for their outing, Margaret, Henry, Catherine, and Sarah made their way to the lake via horseback.

Once there, they set up their blanket on the bank of the lake. Margaret and Henry sat down on it to talk while Sarah went with Catherine to walk along the waterline.

"We are beginning to feel like a real family."

He glanced over at his sister, who was wading in one of the naturally made pools of the river. Then he looked back at Margaret. "Yes, I am beginning to feel the same way."

She wanted to bring up Catherine's introduction to society, but she did not know how to go about it. Worst of all, she feared Henry's anger at her for going behind his back to prepare Catherine.

Margaret was afraid that he was going to be so unraged that he would refuse to even consider it. So, even though Catherine had been ready the last week, she had said nothing, waiting for the right moment.

"I am glad that you are settling in and accepting everything. Once you are fully accustomed to Brookehaven, I was hoping that you would not mind if we hosted a ball. How does that sound?"

She thought about it a moment and realized that it would be the perfect opportunity to introduce Catherine. As her plan began to take shape, her excitement grew. "That would be wonderful, Henry."

"Good, then we shall set the date for two weeks from tomorrow and have the invitations sent out posthaste."

CHAPTER 15

*P*reparations for the ball consumed Margaret's day while Henry consumed her nights. She never thought she could feel so much so deeply for anyone; sometimes it frightened her. She did not like being dependent upon anyone, and the way he made her feel, she knew she was fast falling helplessly in love with Henry. She knew she would never be the same again.

The two weeks passed by swiftly, and before she knew it, the evening of the ball had arrived.

"Are you sure this is the best idea? I mean, not telling Henry about our plans for tonight?"

"Well, I had planned on telling him beforehand, but there never seemed to be the right opportunity." Margaret tucked one of the folds on Catherine's dress.

It was quite possible the loveliest dress that any dressmaker had ever made. The satin dress was in a soft hue of yellow with tiny flowers embroidered all over. It had pieces of gold woven in that shimmered when Catherine moved. It flared out and cascaded down in gentle folds and layers.

Margaret was wearing a less extravagant dress. She had purposely picked one that would subdue her natural beauty and keep Catherine as the focus of the night. She wanted Catherine to be in the spotlight, so she specifically chose not to have a dress made for the evening. She just picked one of the new pale pink ones Henry had given her for a wedding present.

"I hope he does not get angry at us for not saying anything to him. I hate it when Henry gets angry with me."

Margaret laughed as she asked, "Has Henry ever gotten angry with you, Catherine?"

Catherine squeezed her lips together, as she had finally stopped her habit of biting her lip, then replied, "Well no, but there is always a first time for everything. Besides, I have seen him mad at other people, and I would hate to feel his anger directed at me."

"If anyone is going to feel Henry's wrath, it is going to be me. Now, stand still so I can get the final touches finished to your hair."

The young girl's hair was full of ringlets, half piled up and the rest cascading down her slender back. In addition, artfully pinned throughout her hair were tiny flowers that perfectly matched the ones on her dress. She also wore Margaret's yellow topaz set of drop earrings and necklace, giving Catherine the finishing touches to her ensemble.

"I still do not understand why you insist on getting me ready and would not let any of the servants."

Margaret moved a ringlet and pinned it into place. "I have already told you it is because the servants gossip, and I do not want anyone finding out about you, especially Henry."

"Oh, I understand that, but—"

She was cut off when Margaret put her finger over her mouth and beckoned for Catherine to be quiet.

She whispered to her, "I hear someone coming. I want you to go to my other room and shut the door. Do not make a sound." She shoved her lightly. "Go, now."

Catherine ran quickly to the door and went through it, pulling it quietly shut behind her.

Margaret watched to make sure she was hidden and then made her way to her vanity. She sat down and pretended to be prepping herself for the evening.

When the door opened, she glanced in her mirror. It was Henry. She stood up and turned around to greet him.

He looked her up and down and smiled. "I know that dress. I picked it out myself. It looks lovely on you, but is it not a little plain for the hostess of the ball? Why did you not have a seamstress make you a dress?"

She shrugged, not mentioning the fact that the dressmaker had thought he had made a dress for her, but Henry's sister was currently wearing it. Instead, she replied, "I decided to wear this one because I though it enhanced my natural beauty."

"Since you put it that way, I have to agree. It is very

simple, but it does make you even more beautiful, if that is possible. But then, perhaps, I am biased."

Margaret smiled at him, replying, "You had better get ready yourself."

"You are right. I just wanted to come by and check on you to see how things were going. You have been so nervous these past two weeks, even more nervous than when you turned sixteen and went to your first ball."

"That is because this is the first ball I have planned as Viscountess Rolantry. If anything goes wrong, it is I who looks bad."

He kissed her lightly on the forehead. "Nothing will go wrong. You always have everything under control."

With that he turned and left the room.

She sighed after she heard the click of the door and then rushed over to where Catherine was hiding. She opened the door, saying, "It is clear now. You can come out."

Catherine cautiously came out of the other room. "That was close, Margaret."

"It does not matter now. In an hour, you will be on a road from which you cannot turn back. Are you sure you are ready?"

Raising her head, Catherine squared her shoulders. "I am."

"Good. Now I must leave to greet the guests. In an hour, I will come to get you. Then we will present you to the whole world as our sister."

Margaret made her way downstairs to the receiving line

for their guests, and of course, Baron and Baroness Wollingleer were first to arrive.

"Good eve, Lady Helen and Lord Marcus. I am glad that you could make it."

"So are we, Lady Margaret."

Next to arrive was Margaret's father, who gave her a kiss on the cheek and said, "I am glad that you and Henry decided to have this ball tonight. It makes an old man happy to see his only child doing so well."

"I am so glad you could make it, Father. I have missed not being with you every day."

"Well, you know you would see me more often if you came to church once in a while."

Margaret sighed and chose to ignore her father's admonishing comment, instead saying, "We have been so busy, Father."

"Promise me that, once things have settled down around here, you will make an effort to start coming back to church."

"I will do my best."

"That is all I ask. Now I will get out of your way and let you greet the rest of your guests."

As the rest of the ton arrived, Margaret found herself unable to give her undivided attention, as she was focused on Catherine and what was to come next. Margaret made her greetings like a robot with a perfect smile permanently plastered on her face. Meanwhile, her mind was on

Catherine and how she was going to pull this whole thing off.

It had seemed so easy in theory when she first began her quest to introduce Catherine. But now, fear that it was not going to go as smoothly as she had thought began to creep into her thoughts.

Once the receiving line was through, Margaret excused herself from the room and went upstairs to find Catherine.

When Margaret got there, Catherine was not where she had left her. She went into the next room and found her there taking off her ball gown.

"What are you doing?"

"I cannot do this, Margaret. I feel like I am lying, and I do not think I can succeed in this plan."

"You are not lying. You *are* Henry's sister." She touched the girl's arm lightly. "And now you are mine as well."

Catherine looked at Margaret and asked, "Why is this so important to you?"

"It is important to me because you are a good person, Catherine, and I think it is something you need to do. I had a brother once, so I know how important it is to be able to claim your connection to Henry. My brother is lost to me, but yours is right out those doors and downstairs. All you have to do is walk out there and accept what we are offering you."

"*You* are offering me this. My brother has no idea what we have planned for tonight. He may not even want to claim me."

"How many times must I reiterate that at least of this I am certain—Henry loves you and would claim you as his legitimate sister if he thought it at all possible."

They stood there for several seconds without saying anything. Then Catherine said softly, "Perhaps you are right."

Margaret smiled. "Here... let me help you put your gown back on."

Once Catherine was dressed again, Margaret took her by the arm and guided her out into the upstairs hall and around the corner from the main staircase. Margaret had just asked one of the servants to go find Albert, the family butler who had followed her to Brookehaven per her father's instructions. She trusted him with her life and knew that, if she had him announce Catherine to all their assembled guests, he would do it discreetly for her with a little prodding.

"It is about time, Catherine. I will explain everything to Albert. Then I will go find Henry and make sure we are at the bottom of the stairs. It will seem as if both of us planned this, and he will not be able to do anything about it until after the ball. Are you ready?"

Catherine nodded.

"Good, because Albert is coming just now."

Margaret turned to face the elderly butler. He stopped dead just a few feet away, taking in Catherine's appearance.

"My lady, I hope you do not mind me asking, but why is the girl dressed like that?"

Giving Albert one of her most charming looks, she replied, "I was just about to tell you. You are aware that Lady

Catherine, Henry's sister, was away at boarding school and has only recently returned to Brookehaven so that she can find a fiancé?"

"Pardon my ignorance, my lady, but I was unaware that Henry had a sister. I thought he was an only child. We were told that she was a distant relative."

"My husband kept her identity quiet because he wanted to let Lady Catherine get reacquainted without any pressure. The late viscount and viscountess wanted everyone to believe Lord Henry was their only child as they did not want to be bombarded with suitors. They wanted to let Lady Catherine grow up free from family obligations."

Skeptical but not wanting to argue with her, Alfred stated instead, "Lady Margaret, your explanation still does not explain why she is dressed in a ball gown."

"I planned tonight as her introduction into society. I want you to introduce her to our guests."

Albert frowned. "The master will not like this at all."

"But Catherine is his sister and she is already sixteen. She needs to be introduced into society so that she can find a suitable husband. Time is of the essence when it comes to that. Being away from here all these years has already set her at a disadvantage, but this evening will help rectify the situation. If Henry is angry about it, I will take full blame. I will tell him that I ordered you to do this."

"Is it an order, my lady?"

She paused for a moment and then answered, "Yes."

He raised his shoulders in acceptance. "Then I will do

your bidding. When do you want me to make this announcement?"

"Thank you. I will go down to find Henry and position us. Give me ten minutes."

"As you wish, my lady."

Turning, she went down the staircase and weaved her way through the crowds, making acknowledgments along the way as she looked for Henry. She found him near the front doors, talking to several guests.

She came up to him and put her hand on his arm.

Henry smiled down at his wife, saying, "So there you are. I had wondered where you had gotten off to."

Smiling politely, she asked, "May I have a word with you for a moment?"

He turned to the guests he was entertaining and excused himself.

Once they were alone, he asked, "What is it, my love?"

"I have a surprise for you, Henry! I do hope you like it."

"What is it?"

"You have to come with me to find out."

"Is this not a little bit of an inconvenient time? What about our guests?"

"They are going to see it too, but you have to come with me."

He laughed and said, "All right, you win. Lead the way."

Taking his hand, she guided him over to the bottom of the staircase. After a few seconds ticked by, Albert appeared at the top of the spiral set.

Henry looked at her and whispered, "This is my surprise? I have seen Albert a hundred times."

She pinched him playfully and replied, "No, this is."

Albert cleared his throat. "Ladies and gentlemen, assembled guests of the house of Rolantry, it is my pleasure to introduce the daughter of the late Viscount and Viscountess Rolantry, sister to the current Viscount and Viscountess Rolantry. May I present Lady Catherine."

With that, Catherine walked from around the corner and stood at the top of the stairs. There were several gasps, and then everyone began to whisper.

Henry kept his composure. He did not even turn to look at Margaret in surprise, but she felt his grip on her hand tighten to an almost unbearable amount.

Catherine made her way down the stairs and stopped just short of her brother.

She smiled and asked, "What do you think, my lord?"

He looked at her without showing any emotion and replied evenly, "You look lovely."

"Thank you, my lord."

All of a sudden, a flock of people surrounded them, and it was not until an hour later that everyone had met the newest Rolantry member.

Once in the ballroom, Catherine made her way over to Margaret and whispered to her sister-in-law, "My whole dance card is filled up and men are still asking me to dance."

"See, I told you that you would be a success."

"Thank you so much! This means the world to me, and it is more than I could have ever imagined or hoped for."

"I am glad that I could do this for you."

A young nobleman came to claim his dance with Catherine as Henry approached them.

As she watched the couple make their way onto the dance floor, she held her breath as the orchestra started the first dance, then sighed as Catherine fell into perfect step with the young man.

She then turned to face Henry, who had also been watching his sister with the young nobleman.

Grabbing her by the arm, he pulled her out onto the dance floor while saying, "I thought we might dance as well."

He gripped her firmly around the waist, as if anticipating that she might try to flee, thinking he was angry.

Trying to explain quickly, worried that he would erupt at any moment, Margaret began. "I know that you must be terribly upset, Henry. But I did it for both of you. She deserves this and so do you. Look at her. She is *so* happy."

He scowled at her for several moments without saying anything. Then, giving in to his wife, he chuckled and replied, "I was really angry when I found out that you had done this all behind my back. But once I thought about it, I realized that if you had asked me, I would have said no. You may have not been perfectly within your rights to do this, but you did have the right motives." He smiled at her. "And I concede your point—she does deserve this. I have never seen her happier."

As they danced the rest of the cotillion, Margaret informed Henry of what she told Albert to convince him to announce Catherine. When the song ended, he led her off the dance floor.

Baron and Baroness Wollingleer rushed up to them. Barely taking a breath, the baroness asked, "Why did you never tell us about her, Henry, and why are we not her godparents?"

"My parents kept her a secret because they did not want to bother with unwanted people asking for betrothal contracts. They had me taken care of, and they wanted her to be able to choose a love match. It was my father's idea to send her away for school because he wanted her to have a broad learning experience. My parents decided that they were going to let her decide, when she was of age, who she wanted to marry. She only came home a few weeks ago because she was turning sixteen and it was time for her to make that choice."

"Still, over all these years, I thought that one of you would have mentioned her."

He grinned. "She was our best-kept secret. We planned to reveal her at just the right time. Unfortunately, my father died before he saw his plan fulfilled."

Pulling Margaret against his side, he grabbed her hand. "Margaret actually planned everything and decided to introduce her into society this way. Do you approve?"

They could not say no, so instead the baron said, "It was a

grand way to introduce her. Of course, we support you in whatever you decide to do."

Once they were gone, Margaret turned to Henry and said, "You did a superb job of telling Catherine's story, and now it will circulate without you having to retell it over and over. Lady Helen will see to that."

They both laughed. Then Henry bowed and said, "I think I will go claim a dance with my little sister. Thank you, Margaret. You are a wonderful wife."

She watched as her husband went up to Catherine and bowed before her. She curtsied in return. He said something and she laughed lightly. Then he took her hand and led her onto the dance floor.

They made a beautiful pair, the two of them. Margaret sighed and turned around to get a fresh breath of air before anyone tried to claim a dance. She walked over to the glass doors that led to the veranda and went through them.

Margaret decided to go for a walk in the garden. She wanted to sit and relax for a while before she went back inside, having been tense from planning Catherine's big night.

She was glad everything turned out for the better. Of course, the night was not over, but she was not going to think about that. She was satisfied in knowing that both Henry and Catherine were happy and it was in large part due to her.

Finding a deserted bench towards the back of the garden, she decided to sit down for a bit. She leaned against a tree that was directly behind it and sighed as the tension left her body.

"It seems I have great luck finding you alone, little one."

Sitting up straight, she turned her head to the left. Richard was standing a few feet away. He appeared to look somewhat pulled together compared to the last time she had encountered him in the woods, but she could tell by the way he was staring at her that he was still obsessed with winning her back.

"It seems that way."

Coming to sit down next to her, he took her hand into his own. "I came because I had to see you. It has been over a month since I last saw you, and yet you make no attempts to contact me."

She narrowed her eyes. "Why would I? I am married now, my lord."

He glared at her. "So, it is 'my lord' again?"

Pulling her hand away from his grasp, she replied, "I am afraid so, Your Grace. I have decided to accept my situation. I have realized that I can be happy with the way things are and, even in some cases, enjoy it." She pleaded with him, "I beg you, move on and forget about me."

"What about the connection between us"

She licked her lips. "It no longer exists."

Grabbing her by her forearms, he pulled her towards himself. "You are wrong. There still is something between us, and I will show you."

Richard kissed her with an overwhelming amount of

suppressed anger. She shook her head back and forth, not wanting to compromise herself again.

Pulling her mouth away, she gasped, "No! Stop! I cannot do this." Angry that he did not seem to listen to her pleas, she spit out in a whisper, "I have my honor to protect, and you are continuously taking me down a path that will destroy it."

Jumping up from the bench, she started to move away, but before she could escape, Richard grabbed her and pushed her against the nearby tree. He traced kisses over her near-bare shoulders and then worked his way over to the base of her neck.

Margaret focused her strength. Putting her hands between them, she pushed him away. "No! I mean it. I will not compromise this time."

Moving away from his penetrating stare, Margaret walked to the corner of the path. Pausing only for a moment's hesitation, she turned back around and said, "I am sorry, Richard, but I cannot see you again. Please respect my wishes and leave me be."

"You know you want this as much as I do. You can try to deny it, but the attraction will always be there between us." He grabbed her roughly by the arms and seared her with an overpowering kiss.

Something snapped inside Margaret, and she could no longer stand the duke's advancements. She realized that he was selfish and the feelings she once had for him were gone. Without thinking, Margaret yanked away, reached out, and slapped the duke soundly across the face.

She saw a look of astonishment and then rage cross his face.

"Whatever was between us, it is over! You might want to consider moving back to London since there is nothing here for you anymore. I never want to see you again!"

With those final words, she turned and ran from the garden.

Still shaking from her confrontation with the duke, Margaret slipped in through the side veranda doors and discreetly made her way to her chambers. Once in her room, she sat at her vanity and felt herself go limp.

Who was that man who attacked her in the garden just now? She had no idea who the duke truly was or why he continued to be so obsessed with her. Any normal man would accept that she was a married woman and there was no future for them. But the duke continued to pursue her even against her protests. Was he still trying to seduce her to get at Henry? Had that been his plan all along as Henry had insisted?

She had to pull herself together and get back downstairs before someone noticed she was gone. Margaret turned to look at herself in the mirror and quickly fixed what was out of place, not wanting to give anyone a reason to gossip about her appearance.

Once composed and looking like her dignified self, Margaret returned to the ballroom and searched for her husband. He was talking to her father and gestured for her to come over.

"Margaret, your father was just telling me how pleasantly surprised he was to meet my sister, Catherine, for the first time."

"Do you mind dancing with your father one time?"

"Not at all, Father."

The earl took Margaret by the arm and brought her out onto the dance floor. As they glided to the music, he smiled and said, "You know, Henry's father and I had many private conversations, and I remember him mentioning Catherine. We only spoke of it once, and he told me I was the only person with whom he ever discussed the matter."

Margaret felt her mouth go dry as she realized that her father might be getting ready to discredit their charade.

"Is that so? I was under the impression no one knew about Lady Catherine."

He chuckled and said, "Indeed, no one ever knew of 'Lady' Catherine, but I know that Melody, his servant, gave him a daughter and that he loved both of them very much. It troubled him greatly that he could not openly claim them as his family, and we talked in length about his guilt over the entire situation."

Margaret asked in a scared whisper, "Are you going to reveal the truth to everyone?"

"I cannot say I completely approve of what you two have done regarding the girl, but I will stand by you and keep your secret." The earl winked at his daughter and added, "After all, that is what family does. We protect our own, and Catherine is Henry's family in every way that matters."

"Thank you. I am glad that I have you on my side."

The earl stumbled a bit and said, "It seems that I am a bit winded. I am, after all, an old man."

"You are not *that* old, but if you feel you need to rest, I understand."

Margaret took her father over to some of the chairs surrounding the dance floor and helped him sit.

"I need to make sure I talk with all of my guests."

"Of course, daughter. Do what you need to do."

After the ball was over and all their guests had left, Margaret and Henry went upstairs to their rooms and prepared for bed.

"The evening went well. I was surprised that no one really questioned her claim—well, except my father, who promised to keep our secret as he already knew the truth."

Henry looked at her with raised eyebrows as he undid his bow tie and replied, "Well, I am glad that your father is on our side. Regarding everyone else and their lack of observation, we both know that the ton is like a herd of cattle: you only have to usher it in a direction and it will continue to go that way until something changes its course."

She smiled and agreed as she pulled off her shoes. "That is true, so we had better make sure the herd continues to go the way we have prodded them." Margaret rubbed her feet as she asked, "What were all those young men talking to you about?"

He chuckled. "Most of them were asking me if Catherine was betrothed."

"And what did you tell them?"

"I told them that we had not been able to find anyone good enough for her yet."

They both laughed and Henry lifted Margaret into his arms. "You make me so happy. I am a fortunate man to have you as my wife."

Bending her head back in great gasps of pure laughter, she asserted, "You? You must be joking. It is the other way around."

She kissed him on the lips and nuzzled in the crook of his neck. "I am so content when I am with you."

He took her into the bedroom and put her down on the bed. He got down on his knees before her and looked her in the eyes.

"I want to do more than make you content. I want you to want me. Do you?"

She sat completely still for several seconds before saying with obvious fake disdain, "No, I do not! As a matter of fact, I hate your very touch." She crinkled her nose and continued, "But perhaps you could change my mind."

Catching on to her game, he replied, "Whatever it takes, I am willing to try."

"Well, I think you will just have to have a go at it."

He raised his eyebrows and smiled. "Agreed. I will make my best attempt to make you want me."

"All right, when are you going to start trying to persuade me?"

He pushed her back on to the bed. "Now."

CHAPTER 16

*T*hree weeks had passed since the ball. Margaret, Henry, and Catherine had begun to fall into a normal family routine. They spent their mornings apart pursuing their own personal itineraries. Then they usually spent their afternoons together riding, going on picnics, or playing croquet in the garden, and they always had supper together each evening. Margaret finally felt at home with her new husband and sister. She immensely enjoyed the time she spent with them.

She was also beginning to realize that she was having stirrings of wanting children soon, a fact that she had not yet discussed with Henry. But she was thinking, maybe by the end of the year, they could put serious effort into the pursuit. She had even found time to work with the horses, researching the breeding patterns and techniques as well as deciding which stock she wanted to make her trademark.

She was so happy now and wondered how she ever thought she would want another life.

Margaret was reading one of her books about horses in the parlor when she looked up to see Henry approaching her. She stood up from the windowsill bench with a puzzled look on her face, as she could tell something was dreadfully wrong by the deeply sullen look on her husband's face.

"What… what is it?"

He gently touched the side of her face, then said, "I think you should sit down."

Obediently, she followed Henry over to the sofa and sat. Looking at him anxiously, she said, "Tell me."

Walking over to the bar, he poured two glasses, one of brandy for her and one of scotch for himself. He leaned on the counter for a moment, then turned around and made his way back to Margaret, giving her one of the glasses and sitting beside her. "I think you should take a drink."

Ignoring his request, she held the drink in her hand without taking a sip. "What is it, Henry? You are scaring me."

"It is your father." He paused for a moment, taking a strong swig of his scotch, and then continued, "I am so sorry, Margaret, but he passed away last night."

She sat there for several seconds with no reaction except the blinking of her eyes. Without saying a word, she stood up, placed her undrunk glass of brandy on a nearby table, and walked over to the window. She sat on the windowsill bench again and stared out in the direction of her family home.

"How did it happen?" she asked in a monotone voice.

"It was in his sleep. The doctor said he went quickly."

"Do they know what caused it?"

"Apparently, he had been suffering from consumption for some time. The doctor said he had known for at least six months, but your father never told anyone. He had been fighting it on his own and was doing well, but the last few weeks it had been getting worse again. Last night, he went to bed early and no one thought anything of it. His butler found him in the morning."

"Why did he not say anything to me about his condition? He was sick for over six months and never told me," she asked, her voice raw with hurt. Then she remembered that, while at the ball she hosted three weeks prior, her father had gotten sick while they danced and had blamed it on his age. He must have chosen to use that excuse rather than tell her the truth of his condition.

Henry stood and walked over to stand behind her. Putting his hands on her shoulders, he said, "I suppose he did not want to worry you."

She rested her hand on the window and said quietly, "I did not even get to say goodbye."

He turned her around and forced her to look him in the eyes. "He knew that you loved him. You did not have to tell him goodbye. He knew everything he needed to know when he was alive." He wrapped his arms around her as she tried to hold back the tears. "Be reassured that he died knowing you loved him."

~

Margaret felt ill. She knew she had to attend her father's funeral, as everyone expected her to go, but all she wanted to do was sit by the windowsill and think about nothing.

She looked in the mirror and noticed how pale she was. Margaret had looked that way on her wedding day but for a very different reason. How silly she felt over how she had acted back then. She now realized that her father had been sick at the time of her wedding and done what he did because he wanted to make sure she was securely married in case he died. He had said that Henry would make a good husband for her, and he had been right. Her father had always looked out for her best interest, and she had treated his caring actions with defiance.

Her black dress was subdued, with long sleeves and a full skirt. In her hand, she had a black bonnet with black feathers and a mesh veil that she would wear at the graveside. The only touch of color was her mother's cameo that she wore at the top of her collar.

Placing the hat on her head, she pinned it into place. She hated getting ready for her father's funeral. His death brought back all the memories of losing Randall. When he was gone, all she had left was her father. He had become her whole world, and even though she was married and had a new sister, it did not lessen the pain in any way.

She had not let herself cry, partly because she was numb

and partly because she was afraid that if she started crying, she would never stop.

"It is time to go to the funeral, Margaret."

She gave him her hand as he helped her up from her vanity.

"I know this is difficult for you. When I lost my parents a year ago, it was devastating. It is hard to put one foot in front of the other, let alone think about trying to move on without someone you love, but you are strong and I am here for you. I am always here for you, my love."

Margaret turned to her husband and said, "Let us just get through this funeral. I cannot think about anything else right now."

On the carriage ride to the church, Margaret closed her eyes and tried to block out the pain she was feeling inside. She hurt so deeply that she was afraid the ache would never end.

She knew Henry wanted to be there for her, and she wanted to let him, but nothing seemed to help her. Why did everyone she love leave her?

"We are here, Margaret."

Henry got out of the carriage and helped her out as well. Taking her hand and placing it on his arm, he said, "Lean on me if you need to."

Margaret walked towards the church without saying a word. She looked up and realized that the last time she had been there was for their wedding. What she would not give to be able to go back and do that day over, knowing what she knew now. She hated the choices she had made and the damage they had done.

When she opened the doors, Margaret entered a room filled with everyone she knew, and they were all looking at her as they had on her wedding day. But instead of joy and excitement, they wore expressions of sorrow and pity.

Henry helped her to the front pew of the church and they sat down together. She saw the casket sitting open in front of them. As she looked at her father's motionless body, she kept waiting for him to open his eyes or breathe. It was incredibly difficult seeing her father lying lifeless in the cold wooden casket. He had been so full of life that it was odd to see him unable to move.

After a few moments, she saw an older gentleman in an outfit that looked similar to what Reverend Portman would wear. He had carrot-red hair and friendly green eyes and gave her a sympathetic smile as he approached the front podium.

She thought it odd that Reverend Portman was not there but then remembered her father had mentioned that someone named Reverend Fisher had taken over the church. Margaret tried to focus on what he was saying, but her mind felt foggy and everything sounded as if she were underwater. In silence, she sat and waited for the funeral service to be over.

She was not sure how much time passed, but after a while, she felt Henry's hand under her elbow and he was lifting her off the pew.

"We need to go out to the graveside now, Margaret."

Nodding, she allowed herself to be escorted out. She could feel everyone's eyes on her as they made their way into the graveyard outside the church. Once they reached the burial spot, they stood and waited for the pallbearers to bring the casket from the church.

She watched as it passed her by and was placed next to the hole they had already dug. She hated the idea of letting them put him in the ground. Her mind knew it had to happen, but she could not convince her heart to let him go.

As they started to lower the casket into the ground, Margaret wanted to grab the pallbearers and stop them or scream at the top of her lungs to take their hands off his casket, but she did neither. Instead, the sickening feeling returned and the ground beneath her feet felt as if it were going to swallow her whole. She began to shake and sway all at the same time, and before she knew what was happening, she was falling backwards into a blissful sea of nothingness.

It had been two weeks since Margaret had fainted at her father's graveside. Henry was going crazy trying to figure out how to reach her. Margaret had isolated herself into her own world. He wanted so badly to pull her out of her despair, but she just kept pushing him away.

Henry loved her so much, and it was killing him seeing her like this. It was as if the life had been sucked out of her.

She was barely functioning, if you could even call it that. All she did all day was sit by the windowsill and stare outside. It was as if she were waiting for something and searching for something all at once, and he had no idea what.

While he pondered his next move, Catherine entered the room. After watching him for a few minutes, she approached her brother and interrupted his thoughts. "I think that we have been going about this all wrong. We have been trying to reach her separately, but I think we would have a better chance if we tried to reach her together."

He glanced up at his sister and then back down at the floor. "Why should I even try anymore, Catherine? She has banished me from her world. She does not even acknowledge me when I am in the room."

She sighed. "I know. She does the same thing to me, but I think it has to do with the fact that everyone she has ever loved in this world has died—first her mother, then her twin brother, and now her father. I think she is feeling so much pain inside right now that she just exists without allowing herself to feel or think. She is probably afraid that it will overwhelm her if she feels even a little bit."

Catherine put her hand on his arm. "Henry, I think she is pushing us away right now because she is afraid that, if she lets us in, she will lose us too."

"I understand that, but it feels as if it is hopeless. I have been trying to get through to her for the past two weeks and I cannot. She does not eat, she does not sleep, she does not even cry. All she does is sit by that window!"

She frowned. "Perhaps we need to understand better. Why does she sit by that window all day long?"

He looked up and raised his eyebrows in puzzlement. "I have not the foggiest idea." He paused for a moment, and then a new thought occurred to him and he finished, "But I know who does." He clasped his hands together in anticipation. "Now we are getting somewhere." He looked at his sister. "I want you to go find Margaret's companion, Sarah. If anyone would know, it would be her."

"Good thinking, brother. I will go find her immediately." With that, Catherine rushed out of the room to go find the one person who might have the answer.

He was glad that they were finally going to get to the bottom of this and get through to his wife. He loved her, and he was not going to stand by as she self-destructed.

Hearing the door open, Henry turned to find Catherine walking in with Sarah. She looked a bit nervous, and she quickly asked, "What is it you wish to see me about, my lord? I need to get back to Lady Margaret."

Henry waved off her request. "It is about Lady Margaret that I wish to speak to you."

His wife's companion stared at him without saying anything. He continued, "Why does she sit by the window all day?"

Sarah paused, as if not wanting to betray her mistress by revealing the details of her past pains.

Noticing the anxiousness and frown Sarah wore, he

added, "Margaret would want you to tell us what you know. You are the only one who can help us help her!"

Appearing reluctant, Sarah finally replied, "When her twin brother died, she sat by a window in Davenmere without ceasing. She reacted almost the same way, but this does not make sense. You see, he died in a shipwreck off the coast of France. She told her father that he was not dead because she would have felt it. So she sat by the window, waiting for him to return. Why she is sitting there like that now is beyond me. But I sit with her day and night because she is my mistress. *I* will not abandon her." She glared at Henry pointedly.

He realized that from Sarah's point of view it must seem like he had deserted Margaret because he had not spent much time with her since he brought her home from the funeral. The truth was that up until today, he felt that there was really no hope. But this new information helped a great deal.

"Thank you, Sarah. You may return to Lady Margaret. And fear not, for I will be up shortly to check on her."

Sarah nodded and turned around and left the room.

"It is easy to see that she is not pleased with you," Catherine said.

"So it seems," he commented absentmindedly.

"What do you plan to do with this new information?"

He smiled grimly. "I plan to flush her out."

Henry made his way to his wife's chambers and knocked on the door. As expected, she did not respond.

Entering anyway, he went to sit next to her on the window seat.

"Margaret?" No response.

"Darling, it is me, Henry." Still no reaction.

With a glance at Sarah, he dismissed her from the room.

"Margaret, I just got a letter from Randall. He is coming home. He should be back any day now."

For the first time in two weeks, Margaret's focus flickered from the window. Her eyes made a darting movement to where his voice was coming from and then refocused on the window.

"Did you hear me? Randall is going to arrive tomorrow."

This time, her eyes found his and did not return to the window.

"Randall is coming home?" she asked in a confused voice.

"Yes, my dear, and you need to come back to us so that you will be ready when he arrives."

A look of puzzlement crossed her face, then anger. "You are lying! Randall was supposed to come home seven years ago, but he never did. He never did! And neither is my father. My father is never coming back. Never!" she shrieked. "Leave me. I want to be alone." She howled, "Just let me be!"

Grabbing her, he crushed her hard against himself. "No! I will never leave you, Margaret. Do you hear me? Never. You are my life, and if you leave me, then my life is over." He held her in his embrace for several minutes as he stroked her hair. "I love you, Margaret. I need you to come back to me. I cannot do this on my own."

She gripped his shirt in her hands as if he were the only thing that could keep her sane. She looked up and whispered with a flustered voice, "Henry?"

He smiled down at her lovingly. "Yes, my love?"

Defeated, she whispered, "Hold me, just hold me."

He pulled her even deeper into his embrace. "Yes, my love. Until forever, if you will let me."

CHAPTER 17

*L*eaning over to serve Margaret breakfast in bed, Henry said, "You look better."

"I feel much better." She stared at the food with hunger. "You did not have to do this. You could have had one of the servants bring it up."

He smiled. "No, I wanted to. I love serving you."

She blushed lightly. "Thank you. It looks delicious."

Chuckling, he said, "Well, that honor goes to Cook. He said he was not about to let the lady of the house wither away."

At first, she tried to eat as daintily as possible, but her hunger overrode her protocol and she began to shovel the food in. She licked her lips between mouthfuls and wiped them with the napkin Henry had provided.

Glancing up from her breakfast, she found Henry still in the room and, in fact, staring at her while she ate.

Margaret blushed again. "Must you really watch me eat?"

He shrugged. "Why not? You are adorable when you eat."

Rolling her eyes, she said, "You must be going crazy yourself to think that."

"Perhaps, but it is true nonetheless."

Turning to exit the room, he stopped suddenly, saying, "Would you like to go for a ride after you finish eating?"

Her eyes shone with excitement. "Yes, I would enjoy that immensely." She knitted her eyebrows together in contemplation. "And would you mind terribly if Catherine came along?"

Henry smiled affectionately. "Of course not. I think that would be wonderful. I will go let Catherine know so she can get ready, and then I will be back to collect you for our outing."

"That will be perfect."

After he left the room, Margaret quickly finished her meal. Once done, she went over to her vanity and began getting ready. She knew that getting some fresh air and doing something she loved would be good for her, but she felt guilty that she was trying to move on with her life so soon after her father's death. She just had to keep telling herself that he would want her to be happy.

When Henry arrived to take Margaret to the stables, she smiled at him and said, "Thank you for asking me to do this. I am so glad I have you to pull me out of my shell and make me live again."

"I love you. That is what you do when you love someone."

Margaret wanted to say she loved him back, but something kept her from it. She knew she was content in her relationship with Henry, and if she admitted it to herself, she could be falling in love with her husband, but the small doubt in the back of her mind kept her from declaring it.

"Let me pin on my hat and we can make our way to the stables." She grabbed her black hat with feathers that matched her black pants and blouse and quickly donned it.

"You look lovely," Henry said as he smiled at her.

"Thank you."

"Come on, I think we should go back to the lake."

"I think that is a great idea."

Henry and Margaret walked to the stables where Catherine was already waiting for them. Catherine gave Margaret a big hug and said, "I am glad that you wanted to go riding with us today. I have missed spending time with you."

"I know, and I with you."

Margaret mounted Charlie and immediately felt at home. It felt good to be doing something that was normal to her before her father passed away. He had been the one to teach her and Randall how to ride, and because of that, she felt like he was with her now.

The wind blew through her hair as she galloped Charlie in the open fields, and she felt some of the pain fall away. Riding was one of the few things that was always able to bring her joy.

When they reached the lake, the three of them

dismounted. Henry looked at Margaret and stated, "I would love to take a walk with you along the lakeshore."

Margaret turned to Catherine, not wanting to exclude her, but Catherine insisted, "Go. I want to sit with my feet in the water anyway."

Henry took Margaret by the hand as she gave Catherine an appreciative smile.

The two of them walked along the water for several minutes without a word, neither needing to say anything as it felt soothing just being in each other's company. Margaret rested her head upon Henry's shoulder and wrapped her arms around his. This was what she needed. It was as if she could breathe for the first time since she lost her father.

"Henry, I am so glad that I have you. My father was right when he chose you for my husband. I wish I could have told him that while he was still alive."

"He knew I made you happy. He told me at our ball that he had never seen you happier than he had that night."

Margaret sighed in contentment and said, "I am glad to hear that. I like knowing he knew I was taken care of before he left this world."

"I want you to feel more than taken care of, Margaret."

"I do, Henry. I know you adore me."

"And that makes me happy."

Looking out over the lake's water, she whispered, "How happy would me giving you a child make you? I had been contemplating the idea of starting a family before my father's death."

Henry stopped dead in his tracks and turned to face Margaret. "Are you serious? You are ready for that step in our marriage?"

Margaret nodded and said, "You are my family now, and I want us to start our own."

Lifting her up, he twirled her around, laughing, and after several minutes, they both fell down to the ground in a fit of joy.

As they gazed up at the clear blue sky, Margaret asked lightheartedly, "I take that as a yes, then?"

"Nothing would make me happier!"

CHAPTER 18

A week after her father's death, a letter was delivered to Brookehaven addressed to Margaret from her father. She had been in no condition to mentally process it at the time, so it had remained unopened until she worked up the courage to read it.

My Dearest Daughter,

I know that this letter finds you in a state of mourning, but I ask you not to grieve on my behalf. I am where I have always wanted to be—with my Lord and Savior, Jesus Christ. I know that you have not allowed yourself to believe in the Lord since your brother's death, and I realize that I have not always been the best example of what God's love should be. I have prayed and can admit now that maybe I made a mistake by putting my promise to Henry's father over the desires of your heart, my dear sweet child. I am not saying that the duke was right for you, but what I am saying is that you deserved a man who believed in God and would lead you spiritually in the right direction. I fear that, although Henry lives a good life, he is not where he should be with God. In the months after your marriage, I noticed you were not attending church regularly as you had when you lived with me. I cannot help but feel I failed you in that regard. That is why I feel it is my duty to tell you how much Jesus loves you and wants you to let Him be a part of your life. He died for you, Margaret, so you would not have to suffer alone. He gave up His life that you might never perish. He rose again and lives eternally. If I could ask you to do one thing in my memory, it would be that you would accept this most important truth and let Jesus be your salvation. In order to do this, I am asking you to go to the church we used to attend together and talk with the new Reverend Fisher. If you do, you will never regret it. There will be tough times ahead, but the Lord will see you through them if you will let Him. Although I prayed in private, never doubt that you were always at the center of my prayers. I love you.

With great hope,
   Your father

The letter struck Margaret with its earnest sincerity. It was hard to think of God right now when she was in so much pain, but she could not let go of her father's last request.

What harm would it cause to go back to the church? It

was a new reverend after all, and she could go and see if things had changed there. Maybe they would have answers to the questions she had.

Margaret had given up on God a long time back, and Henry had never been much of a believer. Granted, he thought the Bible was filled with good principles to live one's life by, but as far as having a relationship with God, he was right there with Margaret. Believing in God was not part of their lives.

She wondered if Henry would go to church with her. All she could do was ask. Finding him in his study, Margaret came in and sat down across from him.

"Henry, I have a subject that I need to broach with you."

Smiling, he replied, "Then by all means speak, my dear wife."

"As you know, I got a letter from my father."

"Yes," he said expectantly.

"In it, he said that he wanted me to...." How was she going to get this out? She knew that Henry was going to think her an utter fool when she told him she wanted to go back to church. She knew that Henry had merely gone to church to keep up appearances with her father.

Trying to rephrase it, she started over. "He thought it might benefit me to talk to the reverend about his death," she finished lamely.

Henry asked, "You mean you wish to go talk to Reverend Fisher?"

Pausing to gauge his reaction, Margaret cautiously

replied, "Actually, I was thinking about going to church Sunday and talking to Reverend Fisher after the service." She paused and took in a deep breath. "I was hoping you would go with me."

Frowning, Henry stated, "You know how I feel about religion, Margaret."

"I meant, would you go with me for support?"

"Frankly, Margaret, I find church a waste of time."

"I know, but I think I need to do this. It was my father's last request."

After several seconds of deep thought, Henry finally waved his hand in appeasement, saying, "If you feel you must go, you have my permission, but I will not be going with you. I have several things I have to take care of that will take me through Sunday afternoon."

"Thank you. I know you do not understand why I need to do this, and honestly, I can say I am not quite sure myself, but I thank you for letting me sort this out."

As Margaret walked out of her husband's study, she masked her feeling of hurt. It bothered her that Henry was unwilling to go with her when she clearly asked for his support. He said he loved her, and sometimes it felt as if he truly meant it, but when he did such selfish things as refusing to help her when she asked for it because he did not see the point, it made her feel unloved.

She wanted to understand why he only put her needs first when it did not conflict with his own desires. Why could he not have spent one afternoon doing something he did not want to do if it was something she needed him to do with her?

Margaret pushed her troubling feelings aside. Maybe she was being too hard on her husband. No man was perfect, and she needed to accept her husband's limitations.

Margaret stood outside the doors to the church she had not set foot in since her father's funeral. She patted at the black mourning dress she was wearing and took a deep breath, then pushed the left door open and stepped inside quietly. She had purposely come late to avoid all of the greeting that went on before service.

She took a seat towards the back just as the last hymn ended.

Reverend Fisher took to the podium as everyone began to sit. He smiled at the congregation and, after several moments' pause, said, "Let us bow our heads in prayer."

Customarily lowering her head, Margaret continued to kept her eyes open. She smiled wryly as she thought back to when she was little and had feared that God would strike her dead if she opened her eyes during prayer. That was when she had naively believed the words of Reverend Fisher's predecessor, who had constantly berated them with hellfire about anything and everything. He had said that God was there to watch them and make sure they did what he wanted, and if they did not, he would make sure to punish them.

She had never understood that. If bad things happening to you were punishments from God, then why had her brother died? He was only a small boy when his ship went down and sharks claimed his life; surely he was unable to really do anything that would warrant such a harsh punishment.

It was not until after her brother's death that she first opened her eyes, both physically and mentally, to the lies that the former reverend had preached at her and all the others that attended church there. When she opened her eyes back then and nothing happened, she decided in that moment it was time to quit going to church.

Her father had fought her constantly about her attendance, and it was a never-ending battle. He would win and she would go for a stint. Then she would stop talking to him in retaliation and he would give up for a while. This went on for most of her life. But she knew, even though he made her go, he could not make her really believe the way he did. Now she discovered he had never stopped praying for her.

She wondered if that was what had kept her safe all those years through all her wild antics: riding horses that most grown men were afraid to ride, riding by herself in the woods that were full of animals and possibly bandits, walking two miles in a snowstorm in order to get the new shoes she had wanted so badly for a tea party. She had always thought she had been lucky, but could it be that her father's prayers had kept her safe?

But if that were the case, then why had Randall died? Why did her father's prayers not protect her brother?

She wondered if she would ever find the answers.

After the prayer ended, Margaret raised her head reluctantly. She feared a long sermon was coming.

"Today, I have prepared a sermon concerning love. Please turn with me in your Bibles to 1 Corinthians 13:4, and stand for the reading of God's Word." The congregation stood together, and then the reverend quoted the scripture.

Margaret inhaled sharply and started to shake slightly. That was her father's favorite passage in the Bible that talked about the attributes of love. He had quoted it to her more times than she could remember. Had Reverend Fisher planned this with her father before his death? Of course not. It had been several weeks since her father's death, and she had told no one she was coming to church. There was no way he could have known she would be there and how this sermon would affect her, unless…. What if…? Could it be that…? No, it was only coincidence. It was the only thing that could explain how the reverend would have known. Or was it? Was it possible that God was real?

"The Apostle Paul talks in these verses about the characteristics of what Christian love should be. Many of us take for granted that God's love for us embodies these attributes. Not one of them or a few of them, but all of them. His love is perfect. But even though He freely gives us this perfect love, many of us turn away from it.

"What we need to realize is that, if we walk openly in

God's love, not only will we feel His love for us, but we will be able to give His love to others. And this is not love by the world's standards, but love by God's standards—perfect, unconditional love.

"This is our highest command from God: to love one another. Yes, there will be times when it will be hard—there are those who seem to be unlovable—but those are the ones who need to be loved the most. If we ask God, He will give us the ability to love them because He will let His love for them pour through us. We are, after all, vessels of the Lord.

"Most of you know that I have an entirely different view from your former reverend as to how to win people into the Kingdom of God. If we preach 'fire and brimstone' to people, they will not receive the Lord. The only way to reach people is by loving them. After all, it was love that motivated Jesus, the Son of God, to come to Earth, sacrifice himself, and separate himself from His Father, so that you and I could feel His love without sin parting us."

Margaret was rooted to her seat. In all the time she had attended church, she had never heard anyone speak out against the commonplace sermons about "fire and brimstone." Truth be known, she had never really studied the Bible for herself because of how awful the previous reverend had made it sound. Why would she want to read a book that condemned and punished?

Was it possible that Reverend Fisher was right, that God wanted to love her regardless of her mistakes and that if she accepted that, she would never have to hear about "fire and brimstone" again? Her father had quoted 1 Corinthians 13 to her many times before, but she had never really understood the message until that moment.

No wonder she did not feel completely loved! Henry could never measure up to the love God could give her. Not only that, but he was using a flawed love that was only held up to the world's standard.

This also explained why it was so hard for her to love Henry. She was trying to do it all by herself, and without God, nobody could love perfectly. She finally got it! It was like riding a horse with the wrong equipment. It would not feel right for the horse or the rider.

Margaret smiled to herself. Today was the beginning of something wonderful. She had no idea when she stepped foot into her father's church that her life would really change. She was so glad that he had written that letter.

Margaret waited for everyone to leave before she approached Reverend Fisher.

"Reverend, sir, you do not know me, but you knew my father."

The Reverend turned towards her with a knowing smile. "Yes, your father, the earl, spoke of you often. He told me you might come someday. He said he had something special planned. I am just sorry that you were not able to come while he was still alive. He would have loved to have seen you here. He prayed for so long that this day would come."

A tear slipped down Margaret's face. She too wished she had not been so foolish as to not have come sooner.

"Yes, I think I will regret it until my dying day that I did not come to know what my father knew until he was already gone."

"So, you are saying that you have received Jesus Christ, then?"

Margaret nodded, replying, "When you said the prayer at the end of the service, I closed my eyes for the first time in prayer since I was a very little girl. I now believe all of what you said. I needed to hear it. While you were praying, I asked Jesus to come into my life, to change me and how I love others."

"I am gladder than you will ever know. Your father meant a lot to me. He took me under his wing when I first got here from seminary. I am honored that God was able to use me to be the one to bring the earl's daughter into the Lord's Kingdom."

CHAPTER 19

*H*enry approached Margaret, whom he had been avoiding often since she started attending church regularly. He did not seem to like the way she was changing. Or more pointedly, that she was changing because of some religious reason as opposed to him being the root of her change.

"My aunt insisted that you come for tea at their estate as soon as possible. She wants to give her condolences." He paused for dramatic effect. "And, of course, fill you in on all the latest gossip that you have missed these past few weeks."

Margaret gave her husband a pointed look and replied, "Of course."

"So what shall I tell her?"

"I suppose an outing would be nice, and her servants do make a lovely cup of tea. Tell her I will call on her tomorrow if it is not inconvenient."

"Good, I will send a message over straightaway."

～

"I hear that you are a countess now and that your father left everything to you via my Henry. Is it true?" the baroness asked with obvious envy and scorn.

Margaret nodded. "Yes, after my brother's death, he changed his will to make me his heir as long as I was married." She did not mention the fact that, due to her father's sickness, his estate had been impoverished and only the title was worth anything.

"How nice to not only be a viscountess but now a countess as well. But then, you also had the opportunity to be a duchess at one time as well, did you not?"

Resisting the urge to retaliate against the barb, Margaret remained still. After a month of trying to change into what God wanted her to be, it was still hard to fight her old nature. She had to remind herself that the baroness only acted the way she did because she was living her life without God's love being at the center. "Yes, well, I suppose I am very content with my current titles."

The baroness scrutinized every aspect of Margaret's appearance. Still being in mourning, Margaret was wearing a traditional black dress that was well made in lace and fine muslin and trimmed in black ribbon. And although Margaret was dressed appropriately, it did not stop the baroness from picking at her once more.

"You still look a little bit under the weather, my dear. Do you really think you should be out so soon after your collapse?"

Margaret raised an eyebrow and replied, "I am feeling well, Lady Helen." Then, almost as an afterthought, she asked, "By the by, where did you hear that I had a collapse?"

"Oh, come, come, girl, it is common knowledge that you were a bit 'off' after your father's passing."

"Please, appease me. Who told you that?"

She sighed. "Why, I heard it from one of the servants. You know how all the *servants* gossip among the estates."

Margaret frowned. She felt like the baroness was hinting at something with that comment. What was she getting at?

"Yes, servants will gossip, but then, so do most of the women we know."

"'Tis true, but servants' gossip is so much more… interesting." She leaned forward to make her point. "And more precise in nature."

"It seems that you are dying to share a bit of information you found out."

Pulling out her fan, the baroness mechanically flicked her wrist. "I heard that a certain young lady has been secretly seeing a certain duke. Her husband, of course, has no idea, but she *is* seeing him on the sly."

Margaret made her best attempt to keep her anger hidden. It seemed that she had been tricked into coming over here. The baroness had no intentions for this to be a social call. This was a discreetly veiled attack, and the baroness was going for blood—her blood.

"Really? Why, I am pretty sure I know *who* you are talking about, but I believe I know the woman a little better than *you*. And let me reassure you that she has not been doing what the servants say she has. On the contrary, she has been avoiding this duke at all costs and it is he who, at every opportunity possible, has tried to seek her out in secret. She is *faithful* to her husband, and I am sure that she would like me to convey that to you."

Narrowing her eyes, the baroness snapped her fan shut. "I am sure that is what she wants everyone to believe, but I have seen them dance together and share stolen glances when they think no one is watching. I also heard that they had a rendezvous at Lady Catherine's ball. They thought no one saw them, but one of the servants had been passing through the opposite end of the garden and saw them in a, shall we say, intimate conversation. There is something between *that* woman and the duke, and if she has not been unfaithful to her husband as of yet, let me reassure you that it is only a matter of time."

Margaret knew she needed to control her rising anger and so, from her newfound faith, she prayed internally. *God, give me the strength not to retaliate against this infuriating woman. I need you to keep me from doing or saying something that I will regret.*

Waving her hand in her face, Margaret said, "It seems, baroness, that you are right. I am feeling a bit under the weather. I think that perhaps I should be on my way." She stood and inclined her head. "After all, my *husband* is waiting for me at *our* home."

The baroness nodded in return. "Give my love to Henry." She smiled one of her fake smiles and added, "Oh, and if you run into the woman we were discussing earlier, mention that if she is not more careful in the future, her husband is bound to find out."

When Margaret returned home from her uncomfortable afternoon with the baroness, she considered going for a ride to clear her head. Not wanting to go alone, she decided to find Catherine and see if she was interested in going with her.

Margaret could think of nothing else but her disastrous teatime with the baroness. She had been unaware that someone had seen the duke approach her in the garden. What scared her more was that he had been intimately touching her, against her wishes of course, but would someone who was passing by know that, or would they have assumed that she had wanted him to be there with her?

Ever since she had found out, she had been praying that God would work in this situation and keep the duke out of her life. She really wanted to make her marriage work, and if she admitted it to herself, she knew deep down she loved Henry. She just wished he would attend church with her and find his own relationship with God. If he did, their life together would be perfect.

She really needed to go for a ride, so she hurried down

the corridor to the library, thinking that Catherine might be reading in there. When she reached the doors to the room, she heard voices on the other side. She waited to hear whose they were.

Margaret recognized the first voice as belonging to Catherine. "Oh, Lord Marcus, you startled me. I was reading Faust and I did not hear you come in. What brings you here, my lord?"

"Why, I came here under the pretense to see your brother, Henry, but I must admit that my real motive was to see you."

"Me? You flatter me, sir, but why do you seek me out?"

Margaret could hear the lechery enter his voice. "Because, my dear, I want to taste the merchandise before your brother sells it off to the highest bidder."

She heard a gasp and a loud slap. Then she heard the baron curse, followed by scuffling and him saying, "I will teach you to slap me, girl! After I am through with you, you will be begging me to stop."

My goodness, that bounder! That cad! Margaret thought. The nerve he had to come into her home and try to take advantage of Henry's sister. She would not stand for it!

Margaret had heard enough. She barged in through the doors, catching the baron off guard with Catherine roughly trapped in his arms.

"I recommend you remove yourself from my sister."

Immediately, he pushed Catherine away as if she were of no consequence.

"Lady Margaret, what brings you here at this precise

time? I was under the impression that you were taking tea with my wife."

So, Margaret thought, *he had planned this whole thing. He knew that I would be away and that Henry was busy with his business affairs. Well, I will teach him to try to take advantage of an innocent girl!*

"Yes, I just returned from being with your wife. I wonder how she would feel to know what you have been up to while you were away. I wanted to go for a ride and was coming to ask Catherine if she wished to go with me, but I can see that you were not expecting *that*. Let me make myself clear, Lord Marcus. If I ever see you making advances towards Lady Catherine again, I will personally see that your life becomes unbearable!" She paused and glared at him. "Do I make myself understood?"

He clenched his teeth and replied with malice, "Quite clear, Lady Margaret."

"Good. Now, I would advise you to leave, quickly if I were you, before I inform my husband of what you attempted to do to his younger sister just moments ago in his own home."

The baron's eyes grew wide with fear. "You are going to tell Henry?"

Margaret tightened her lips. "Of course I am going to tell him. I tell my husband everything."

He snickered with disbelief and replied sarcastically, "Yes, I am sure that you tell him about your dalliances with the duke. I am sure that they make terrific bedtime stories."

She chose to ignore his barb. "I would make haste if I were you. You will not want Henry to catch up to you once he finds out."

A look of sheer panic washed across the baron's face before he rushed quickly from the room.

Catherine turned to face her sister with a look of shock and hurt. "I did not provoke that, Margaret. Honestly I did not!"

Margaret approached her sister-in-law and put her arms around her. "I know you did not. Lord Marcus has always been a lecher. He even made a pass at me one time. He is a horrible man who is married to a horrible woman. And thank goodness they did not have children, because no doubt they would be horrible as well."

Laughing softly, Catherine tried to defuse the awkwardness in the room. "Thank you for intervening. I had no idea that he was going to try something like that."

"Unfortunately, one never knows how someone is going to act, and people with money often think they can get away with anything." She hugged her once more, then released her. "Now I must go inform Henry about what took place."

Still shaking from the ordeal, Catherine implored in embarrassment, "Must you really? I was hoping that we could just forget about it."

Margaret smiled grimly. "I wish that we could, but Henry needs to know so he can keep it from happening again. When it happened to me, I felt as you did and did not tell

Henry, hoping it was an isolated incident. But the baron's misconduct can no longer go ignored."

Catherine nodded in surrender. "Then do what you must."

As Margaret made her way to her husband's study, she thought about what the baron had just done to Catherine. Margaret wished she had done something after he had made the comments he had during her sixteenth birthday. If she had, her sister would not have had to go through what just happened.

Knocking lightly on the study door, Margaret heard Henry say, "What is it?"

"Henry, can I speak with you a moment?" she asked as she opened the door and stepped into the room.

He glanced up. "Can it wait until a little later?" Then he looked back down at his work.

"Actually, no, it cannot."

Pushing the papers away, he stood up. "All right, I suppose I need a break anyway." He came around the desk and sat on the corner of it, giving his undivided attention to Margaret. "What is it?"

She licked her lips. "It has to do with your uncle."

He raised one of his eyebrows in question. "Oh, and what has the old goose done now?"

"He came here just a few minutes ago under the pretense to see you. I assume you know this?"

"I am aware."

"Well, I went to find Catherine to see if she wanted to go

for a ride, but when I got to the library, I found your uncle trying to… take advantage of her."

Henry stood up slowly from the corner of his desk and asked, "Did you witness this?"

She nodded. "I overheard him making a crude sexual comment to her, and then she slapped him. He grabbed her and was about to…." She avoided saying it. "I intervened and told him to leave."

Seeing the rage enter Henry's eyes and the effort he was exerting to try to control it, Margaret knew the baron would be feeling Henry's wrath soon enough.

"I appreciate your intervention, Margaret. Thank you for defending my sister's honor. I will take care of the situation from here."

She turned around to leave, then stopped. "What do you plan to do?"

He looked at her. "It is of no concern of yours."

"But it is, you see, as I feel partially to blame for what just happened to Catherine. If I had said something a long time ago, something like this could have been avoided."

"What are you talking about, Margaret?"

"Your uncle made an innuendo to me at my birthday celebration. I did not tell you because, to be quite honest, I felt embarrassed about the whole thing. Besides, someone interceded and I just wanted to forget the incident." She frowned. "But I want him to stop this. He has no right trying to use young girls for his own disgusting purposes. Who knows who will be next—perhaps our daughter when we have one?"

Henry shook his head. "I do not think so. I plan to make sure he never tries anything like this again."

Going over to his bar, he poured himself a glass of scotch and a brandy for Margaret. He walked back over to her and handed her the drink. She smiled in appreciation as she took it.

"No one knows this, but I have been financially supporting my godparents for the last year. He gambled everything away and had nothing left. Needless to say, Lady Helen has expensive taste and he needed money fast. I loaned it to him and he lost it as well."

He turned around and went back over to his desk. Opening one of the drawers, he pulled out several pieces of legal paperwork. He then handed it to her and continued, "Those papers are the deed to their home and everything else they own. He signed it all over to me as collateral for his last loan. He lost the loan gambling again, and now I own all of it." He grinned smugly. "He will do what I say or I will send them packing."

Margaret sat dumbfounded. She felt like she did not know her husband at all to keep such a secret from her. She wanted to ask him if he "owned" anyone else's life the way he did his aunt and uncle's, but she was afraid of what the answer might be and what kind of person that would make him.

Coldly, Margaret said, "Thank you for taking care of this, my lord. I will be on my way." Angrily, she abruptly swung around to leave the room.

But before she could get away, Henry asked, "I can tell I said something to upset you. What was it?"

She stopped where she was with her hand on the doorknob. She stood there a moment and then turned back around.

"It is only that you seem to have all these secrets that I know nothing about. First, there was Catherine. Now there is this, and I wonder, how many other things are you keeping from me?"

He went up to her and put his hands on her upper arms. "I am not purposely keeping anything from you. I just did not realize that is how it appears. I promise that I do not mean to do it."

"I believe you, but that does not ease my mind."

Looking her in the eyes, he asked, "What would?"

"If you would answer a question for me."

She felt him relax a bit. "What is it?"

"How many other people do you own like that?"

He thought about it for a few moments and then replied matter-of-factly, "Eight."

Her eyes rounded in surprise. "Truly? And are they all titled?"

"Yes, they are all titled. Does that satisfy your curiosity?"

She nodded.

"Good, because I have never told anyone as much as I have told you."

She smiled. "Thank you for trusting me."

CHAPTER 20

Margaret was in the stables helping groom Charlie. She could have asked one of the stable hands to do it, but she found it relaxing to take care of the horses.

"You are such a good girl, Charlie. You make me so happy. When I am done brushing your mane, I will take you out for a run. Does that sound good, girl?"

Charlie neighed in response and leaned into Margaret's hand as she brushed the horse.

"You are a formidable woman, Lady Margaret. I have come to make my apologies to you and Lady Catherine."

When she turned around, she found the Baron Wollingleer standing behind her. He was uncomfortably close, and she could tell he was angry underneath his fake friendly exterior.

"There is no need for apologies to me. Just make sure you

keep from doing anything like it again in the future and everything will be forgotten."

"I wish it were that easy. It seems that my nephew is quite upset with the misunderstandings between all of us."

Margaret glared at him. "There was no 'misunderstanding.' Your intentions were quite clear and atrocious."

"I am sorry you feel that way, Lady Margaret. I was merely paying compliments to a beautiful young woman. I did not see any harm in that."

"Say what you will, but I will not be swayed in what I know you to be about when it comes to young ladies."

Her comment must have struck a nerve because the baron sneered at her and said, "Women should know their places and keep their mouths shut. Their job is to look pretty, bear us children, and run our homes, and in that order. I am not happy that you have jeopardized my family's status with the lies you have been putting in Henry's ears."

"I have not been spreading any lies, Lord Marcus, and I do not appreciate the way you are talking to me right now. Do I need to tell my husband about this conversation as well?"

"It seems all you know how to do is hide behind your husband. Henry may think he can control everyone with his money, but money cannot keep his loved ones as safe as he thinks. There are bandits in the woods you ride in, are there not, Lady Margaret? What is to keep one of them from *attacking* you?"

Margaret sucked in a deep breath and held it. Was Baron

Wollingleer threatening her? If he was, he was doing a good job of veiling the warning, making it difficult for her to confront him on it.

"You are truculent by nature, Lord Marcus, and I do not wish to engage with you. I think it is best if you leave at once. If you go now, I will do you the favor of not telling my husband what you have said here today."

With that, the baron reluctantly turned around and started to leave the stables, but not before uttering one more ominous threat. "I would be careful if I were you, Lady Margaret. You have *no idea* how many enemies you have been making."

Margaret watched the baron's retreating figure and only let her guard down once he was out of sight.

He had implied that she had more enemies than just him. What did he mean by that? Who else had a reason to be her adversary? She racked her memories but could not fathom to whom he was referring.

As Margaret was having Charlie saddled up for her ride, Sarah approached her, saying, "Catherine sent me to ride with you as she has been detained with other matters. She sends her regrets that she cannot go riding with you today."

Nodding in acknowledgment, she said to one of the stable hands, "Please make ready another horse for Sarah."

"I passed Lord Marcus, who seemed to be in a sour mood. Is everything all right, my lady?"

Margaret appreciated Sarah's concern but did not want to talk about her conflict with the baron. "Nothing to worry about, Sarah. He is a toothless lion. Are you ready to go riding with me?"

"Of course, my lady."

Both the women mounted their horses and galloped off towards the lake. She could tell Charlie was happy to be running free, and as always, she also enjoyed the liberty of being out in the open.

As they approached the woods, Margaret became nervous, remembering the baron's earlier threats towards her regarding bandits. But she knew she was being silly. She had grown up riding in these woods, and she had never encountered any problems from strangers. Still, she pulled up on Charlie's reins and lingered on the edge of forest, not sure if she felt like proceeding on the paths going into them.

"What is wrong, my lady? Your favorite part of riding is going into the woods."

Margaret shrugged off her reservations and said, "You are absolutely right, Sarah. You take the lead. I will follow behind."

The forest was full of commotion and Margaret enjoyed hearing the birds chirping, watching the little rabbits and squirrels scurrying through the underbrush, and she even had the pleasure of seeing a deer dash across the path and then jump over a nearby log. She loved living in the country and being so close to nature.

"I think, up at the next watering hole, we should rest the horses before we head back."

"As you wish, my lady."

As they continued to trot along the path, Margaret looked around at the forest and amused herself with the animals' activities. But without warning the woods became eerily quiet, and she noticed that the animals had disappeared. What was going on?

Her instincts told her something unsettling was about to happen. "Sarah, I think we need to turn around right now and get out of here as quickly as possible."

"What is the matter? You seem frightened."

"Something is not right, and we need to leave now!"

But before they could make their escape, Margaret and Sarah saw several men in hooded cloaks emerge from farther back in the forest and surround them.

Margaret and Sarah were frozen with fear. Moments ticked by without anyone saying a word.

Finally, one of the men broke the silence, saying, "It seems you've wandered into our part of the forest, ma'am. I think you need to pay a toll."

"If it is money you are after, I regret to inform you that I never carry any on me when I am riding, nor do I wear any jewels. I have nothing to offer you, and I think it best if you let us leave the way we came. After all, these woods belong to my family and you are trespassing."

"The woods belong to everyone, and you'd be wise to remember that. No one has the right to say they own them, least of all your family. And if you can't pay my toll with worldly goods, I may be forced to take my payment in... *other* ways."

Margaret squirmed in her saddle, very much aware of the way the men were unsuitably ogling Sarah and her.

"Do you know who my husband is? I am married to the Viscount Rolantry, and he will not tolerate bandits accosting his wife and servant."

"We're very aware of who you are. It's why we stopped you in the first place."

Margaret's eyes grew wide with disbelief. How did they know who she was, and why did that make her their target? Had Baron Wollingleer planned this and confronted her in the stables already knowing she would be riding as usual that afternoon?

"Tie up the blonde one against a tree but grab the dark-haired one. She's the one we were told to take."

She began to kick and scream as two men grabbed her and yanked her off her horse. She could hear Sarah screaming as well and heard one of them slap her, saying, "We were told we had to handle your missus with care, but no one said nothing about how we needed to treat you. You best calm down or I'm going to make you wish you had done what I said."

Sarah went quiet in the bandit's arms. But before Margaret could figure out what else they were doing to Sarah, her attention was drawn to her own arms that were being tied in front of her. Just as she was about to object to the rough handling, she was being tossed onto one of the men's shoulders.

Just as quickly as they materialized from the forest, they

faded back into its dark covering. The group of men was running through the forest, causing Margaret to be harshly tussled on the man's shoulder, and she was unable to catch her breath from all the bouncing. She felt as if she were going to be ill from the constant swirling sensations that she was getting from being upside down and moving at the same time.

After some time of the men pushing deeper and deeper into the thickest part of the forest, Margaret struggled to say through her jagged breathing, "We… need to… stop. I think… I am going to be… sick."

"If you're going to be sick, go ahead and vomit. We're not stopping."

Margaret wanted to concentrate on what was going on and why these men had taken her, but a massive headache was forming, and she knew that the only thing she could do was focus on blocking out the pain and not giving them the satisfaction of vomiting.

At some point, Margaret fainted from the throbbing in her head. When she regained consciousness, she was unsure of how long she had been carried on the man's shoulders, as none of her surroundings were familiar. Where were they taking her?

After several more moments, Margaret was crudely dumped on the ground by a small fire in a dirt pit.

Looking around, she noticed that some of the men were missing. But that still left the one she assumed was the bandit leader and another man guarding her, and she knew full well that even if she managed to get to her feet and take off, she would not get far before they caught up with her, especially with her arms tied. And if she ran, once they had her again, they would be angry for her defiance, which would make their treatment of her even worse. Her only choice was to sit and wait for an opportunity to escape without being noticed.

She knew she was most likely safe since she heard them say that someone had sent them to do this and they wanted her unharmed. Quietly she sat with her eyes closed and prayed to God. *Please keep Sarah safe and help me right now. I know you are always with me, and I ask that you help me get out of this situation. I am so scared, so please give me peace and deliver me from this!*

Margaret opened her eyes and asked, "Is my servant all right?"

The still-hooded bandit leader looked at her and said coldly, "She should be as long as someone finds her before the animals do."

Margaret flinched at the thought of such a thing occurring. Sarah had been with her since she could remember, and since her father's death, she had become the only person, besides Albert, who had known Margaret through her entire life. She did not know what she would do if something should happen to Sarah.

"You had better hope nothing happens to her, or I will have your head."

"You're in no position to be making threats, girl. You

would be smart to remember that you're our prisoner and under my protection here in this part of the forest. You wouldn't want to know what would happen to you if I decided you weren't worth protecting any longer."

Margaret swallowed several times, trying to force down the lump in the back of her throat, but to no avail.

"May I please have a drink? I am exceedingly parched and still feel faint."

The leader came over to her and rudely shoved a metal mug of water at her.

She tried to take the mug but was unable to with her hands tied. "Might you untie my hands so I am able to hold the cup?"

"No, I'm not going to do that." Instead, he bent down to her level and put the mug to her lips. "Here, I'll hold it for you while you drink."

Ravenously, she drank from the mug until she was sated. With a bit of curiosity, Margaret timidly looked at the leader, trying to determine if she recognized anything about him. Their eyes met for a brief moment before he stood up, walked to the other side of the fire, and sat down on the ground.

"Not a good idea to get too close to me, girl."

"Why have you taken me?"

"Because someone paid us very well to do so."

"It does not bother you to abduct someone without knowing why?"

"Money's the only reason I need. Your kind has ridden on

the back of my kind for far too long, and it's about time one of you was knocked off your almighty pedestal. My only regret is that I don't get to do this to more of you."

"What are you talking about, 'my kind'?"

"I mean the nobility. You have everything and give nothing to the common people. You think we're here for your every whim and matter as nothing more than that."

"You know nothing about me. I care very deeply for my servants and have always treated them as family."

The bandit leader snorted and said, "You mean you give them your scraps and expect them to be happy for it. Don't try to convince me of how gracious you are to my kind. I worked for people like you, and I was starved and beaten half to death for something I didn't even do. That's why I left and took to the woods. I *know* what you and your kind are."

"Then why are you working for someone like me?"

"And how would you know that?"

"You said you were getting paid handsomely, and only someone who is titled would be able to have access to that kind of money."

"You're a smart one, you are, but being smart isn't going to get you out of this."

The other bandit that had been sitting and listening stood up, went over to the leader and asked, "How long are we staying here?"

"Until *he* arrives to pay us and collect her."

"What does he want with her, anyway?"

"Who cares? Their kind never makes sense."

"Did he give you a time?"

"Does it matter? Like you have somewhere to be. I want you to go out and keep watch with the others. There's a chance they've found her servant by now and are looking for her."

Margaret began to feel a bit of hope. What if someone had found Sarah or she had gotten free and ran for help? There was a possibility there was a search party out looking for her right now, and she knew Henry would not stop until he got her back safe and sound.

"If you are only doing this for money, I can pay you double whatever the person who hired you to do this is paying. I am the Countess of Renwick and my husband will give you whatever you want for my safe return."

"Do you think that just because I'm poor you can buy me off? Unlike your kind, I'm a person of my word. I made a deal and I won't go back on it, no matter what you offer me."

"I did not mean it like that."

He jumped up off the ground and came at her. "I don't care what you meant, and I suggest you quit talking right now. He said you were to be unharmed, but I'm starting to not care about the dock in pay if you have a few bumps and bruises by way of my knuckles."

He raised his fist to her. Margaret cringed in anticipation of what was coming and inhaled sharply, waiting for the blow to land.

"I would not hit her if I were you."

Margaret let out a huge sigh of relief at the sound of her husband's voice.

Startled, the bandit leader spun around to look at Henry and sputtered out, "Who're you and how'd you get past my men?"

"I am the Viscount Rolantry, and that woman over there that you were about to hit is my wife. As for your men, *my* men have secured them and they will be handed over to the authorities for due process. If you are wise, you will surrender yourself as well."

The bandit leader sneered at Henry and spat on the ground between them. "I'd rather die first." He pulled a sword free from his belt.

"So be it," Henry stated as he gracefully unsheathed his own sword.

Jumping to her feet in fear, she said, "No, Henry, let us just leave! I could not stand it if something happened to you!"

"Margaret, as long as he is free, there is a chance they will come for you again. I cannot have that possibility looming over our lives. I am sorry but I must end this."

The bandit leader crouched and started circling Henry like a wolf, looking for an opening to attack. But Henry had been trained in the military, and though he had been out of practice, he was still an expert with the sword. When the bandit leader struck, Henry was ready and quickly deflected it, swinging his sword in return. The two of them exchanged blow for blow for several seconds, with both proficiently blocking and returning thrust for thrust.

"You realize you will be surrounded at any moment. You can end this now before it is too late," Henry offered.

"Your kind would fight unfair, using your superior numbers to overpower me and claim it a victory."

"I am trying to spare your life for the sake of not wanting to shed blood in front of my wife. But once my men arrive, they will not hesitate to end you. That is if I do not kill you first myself."

The bandit leader growled, "You can try," and lunged forward at Henry, who dodged the majority of the attack, but the edge of the bandit leader's sword tore through Henry's shirt on his left arm.

Margaret screamed as blood began to pour from her husband's open wound, but it did not faze Henry who, fortunately, was right-handed. Without warning, Henry skillfully pivoted around and struck at the bandit leader who was caught completely off guard, not expecting such a swift counterattack after landing a blow on his opponent.

Henry's sword pierced the bandit leader's chest. The man slumped forward on it, defeated.

"You think by killing me that your wife is safe? She will never be safe as long as the one who hired me still wants her —" Before he could finish his sentence, the bandit leader started choking on his own blood.

Henry grabbed him by the front of his shirt and asked

with fury, "Who? Who are you talking about, and what do they want with my wife?"

But it was too late; the bandit leader was dead. Henry released him and he fell to the ground in a heap.

Margaret rushed to Henry and gently placed her hand on his arm near his wound, asking with worry, "Are you all right, Henry?"

"Yes, my love. The better question is if you are all right." He put his good arm around her.

"They did not harm me, thanks to you getting here just in time." Then realizing she had no idea how he *had* gotten there, she asked, "How did you find me? Was it Sarah? Is she all right?"

"Sarah is doing well. She is back at Brookehaven. But it was actually Charlie that saved the day. The bandits did not secure her when they took you, and they must not have realized that she had been trained to return to the stables when she was without a rider. When she came back without you, one of the stable hands came and got me immediately. We formed a small search party within minutes and came looking for you and Sarah.

"We found her pretty quickly. She was unconscious and when we got her to come to, she explained what had happened. She was even able to tell us which way they took you. Luckily, Fredrick, one of the stable hands, is an excellent tracker, and we were able to catch up to you with them unaware."

Margaret hugged Henry tightly. "I am so glad you found

me, Henry! I was so scared but somehow, after I prayed, I felt like God would help you find me before it was too late."

Henry did not acknowledge Margaret's reference to God but avoided it by saying: "Let us get you home so you can rest."

"Very well, Henry. Some rest sounds heavenly. But I am still worried about what the bandit leader said before his death. Who do you think was behind this? Just before I was abducted, your uncle threatened me, even mentioned bandits in the woods specifically. Do you think he is capable of this?"

"I am not sure who did this to you, but I intend to find out and take care of whoever it is permanently."

CHAPTER 21

Several days had passed since the bandits in the woods had abducted Margaret. Henry had asked her to refrain from riding until he could find and eliminate the threat against her. And although she loved riding, she had to agree that it was unsafe for her to do so until then.

Margaret spent her free time reading by the window, doing needlepoint, and going for walks in the garden.

It was Sunday and she was getting ready for church. Of course, Henry insisted on sending several armed men with her to keep her safe. She did not argue, trusting in her husband and his decisions.

Catherine knocked on her door. "May I come in, Margaret? I have something to ask you."

"Certainly. What is it you wish to ask me?"

"I want to go with you to church today. Before you argue with me and tell me Henry would not like it, I want to let you know I already broached the subject with him. He told me that if it was what I wanted, he was not going to stand in my way."

A big smile crossed Margaret's face. "I would love for you to come with me. Do you mind me asking why you want to?"

"Honestly, I have seen a huge change in you, Margaret. I do not even know if I can exactly put it into words, but you seem more peaceful and whole since you starting going to church. I thought once my brother claimed me as his sister, I would finally feel complete. But although I am content most of the time, I still feel like something is missing. I want to have what you have."

"Oh, Catherine, I am so happy to hear that! You are going to love Reverend Fisher. He is the wisest man I have ever known, and he truly cares." Margaret hugged her sister. "Let us go downstairs. The carriage is waiting."

On the carriage ride to church, Margaret thought about what Catherine had said. She knew she was changing on the inside every day because of God, but it was an affirmation to hear from someone else that they could see the manifestation of her internal decisions from the outside as well. It was hard at times, and she constantly struggled between doing things the way she used to and doing them the way God would want her to, through His perfect love.

When they arrived at church, everyone was excited to see Margaret and even more surprised to see Catherine with her. Margaret noticed that the Baron and Baroness

Wollingleer were not in attendance. Did that mean Henry had found out that the baron was behind her abduction?

Margaret and Catherine sat in Margaret's normal spot just before Reverend Fisher began his sermon.

"Good morning, ladies and gentlemen. I know I discuss the attributes of love often. It is because God tells us that the most important aspect of His character is His perfect love. How transforming is it that God is willing to not only share that love with us but make it possible that we can share that love with others? We are the vessels God chooses to use to pour out his mercy and love to help others find their way to the Lord. Please stand with me for the reading of God's Word."

Catherine grabbed Margaret's hand and squeezed it tight. Margaret knew her sister-in-law was one step closer to accepting God into her heart. When she did, Margaret would have an ally in helping Henry feel God's perfect love.

No one had seen the Baron and Baroness Wollingleer for over two weeks. Henry told Margaret he was positive that it was his uncle who orchestrated her abduction as retaliation and most likely planned to anonymously ransom her back to him for profit.

Margaret hated that Henry was brokenhearted from his family turning on them. With their disappearance, it confirmed their guilt.

Although still weary from her ordeal, Margaret tried to return to her normal routine once Henry determined that the threat to her life was over. She was in the stables taking care of Charlie when she received a hand-delivered letter from one of the stable hands. He said a servant from Burlingler had dropped it off earlier with specific instructions that only the Lady Margaret was to receive it.

She opened it and read the contents:

Countess of Renwick,

It is urgent that you see me at once. I have information about your husband that would prove devastating to your whole family. Come this evening to Burlingler Estate alone around six o'clock and I will give you the information. If you do not come, then the information will be released to the newspapers. The choice is yours.

The Duke of Witherton

She folded the letter and replaced it in the envelope as she thought about the message. Her intuition told her it was a trap of some sort, but she did not want to take the risk that it was true. She had to follow through and make sure that whatever it was he had dug up on Henry did not get released.

It was possible that he had found out about how Henry "owned" several of the nobles in their county and planned to release the list of names, or worse yet, he had found out about Catherine's true illegitimacy and planned to make that information public. If that information got out, it would ruin them all. She could not be a part of destroying Henry, so she knew she had to meet the duke to keep him from hurting her family. If there was any part of him that still loved her, perhaps she could convince him not to release whatever information he had concerning her husband.

Margaret secretly left the house, taking Charlie as quickly and quietly as possible. She wanted this to be over, and she knew that the sooner she got there, the better.

As she found herself knocking on the door to Richard's estate, she could not believe that she was there. He was Henry's most bitter enemy and her almost-lover. He was a danger to her honor, and yet there she stood like a lamb at the entrance to a wolf's den.

Richard's butler opened the door, saying, "Welcome, Countess. I will tell His Grace that you have arrived."

The cold air rushed across her face as she stood outside. Her cape twisted around her, being pulled in numerous directions, as was her heart.

Richard's butler ushered Margaret in and escorted her to the library. Then he left the room without another word.

Irritably, Margaret tapped her foot on the floor as she stared at the doors, expecting Richard to enter through them any moment. What was keeping him? She did not have the patience for this.

She went over to the bar and poured herself a brandy. She knew it was rude, but she did not care. His butler was rude for not offering her one in the first place, and Richard was rude for not training his butler to do so.

Taking a swig, she felt the burning sensation as it went down. It felt good, and she could tell it was calming her nerves. She finished off the contents and poured herself another brandy. She was about to take another swallow when the door opened and Richard stepped through, shutting it behind him.

She eyed him skeptically for several seconds before asking, "What does this concern?"

He smiled with self-satisfaction. "Patience, my dear. Everything will reveal itself in time."

Glancing at the glass in her hand, he asked, "Would you like another? It will make things a lot easier, I think."

"No, thank you." She sat it down on the edge of the bar. "Will you please get to the point? Why did you send me this letter?" Margaret pulled out the letter and shook it at Richard.

Like a slithering snake, he moved sinuously over to where she stood. He reached out and grabbed the letter from her.

"I needed to see you, and I knew the letter would make you come."

Never taking his eyes off Margaret, Richard took the

piece of paper and threw it into the fireplace. He stared at her for several seconds before reaching out and touching the side of her face.

Instinctively, she flinched and pulled away.

"So, it is to be like that? I feared that this would not be pleasant."

He went to kiss her and she moved her head to the side, asking, "What are you trying to do, Richard? I thought this was about Henry."

"*Henry.* It is always about *Henry* with you these days," he spat. She could smell the overwhelming scent of alcohol on his breath and realized she was in a very dangerous situation, as it was quite apparent that he was intoxicated.

Margaret tried to step away, but he grabbed her arms and yanked her hard against him.

"I hate the Viscount Rolantry! I hate him for stealing my rank and position when we were in the military, for stealing you, but most of all, I hate him for always acting as if he deserves all those things."

He leaned in close to her and continued spewing his venomous spite. "It makes me sick the way everyone looks up to him. He is a lowly viscount who consorts with bastards and peasants. He does not even deserve to be part of the nobility."

Narrowing her eyes and pulling free of his grasp, she stepped a few feet back and said, "Do not insult my husband in my presence, sir! I did not come here for you to take those kinds of liberties." She started to move around him while saying, "I do not know what kind of game you are playing, but I will be taking my leave, *Your Grace.*"

The duke grabbed her, slamming her against the bookshelf and knocking the air out of her.

"I think not. I will take all the liberties I please, and I will take much more than I already have."

With that, his mouth came down on hers, hard and cruel. He tried to get her to respond, but when she would not, he became even more brutal. She tried to twist away from him, but he held her firmly against the bookshelf. She cried out as he pushed her even harder into it and several books' edges dug into her delicate skin, stabbing her in the back and causing sharp pangs to course through her body.

Margaret was pinned against the bookcase by the duke's body as he yanked her head back by her hair and began to grope and touch her in unspeakable places as she sobbed and begged him to stop. She fought against him as he continued to force his unwanted attention on her, but he was so much stronger.

The duke threw her to the ground roughly while she wept uncontrollably. Between sobs, she pleaded, "Please... Richard, do not... do *this*. If you ever loved me... I beg you... my honor, my virtue!"

Ignoring her pleas, the duke leered over her savagely. "I am tired of hearing about your stupid honor. I will destroy it so it will never stand between us again!"

❧

For the rest of her life, she would try to block out the memories of that night, but they would always haunt her, waking her in the middle of the night, causing her to weep with despair.

The moment Richard committed his treacherous act, any of the feelings that Margaret still felt for him vanished, hate replacing them.

She lay crumpled in a heap in the middle of his library floor. Feeling the need to flee, Margaret wobbly stood and quickly pulled at the torn pieces of her dress, holding the top together in her fist. As she headed for the door, Richard jumped up and cut off her escape route.

"Oh no, you do not. I am not finished with you yet." He roughly pulled her tattered dress from her shaking body. Brutally, he grabbed her and forced another kiss upon her. It was at that most awful moment when Henry walked into the room.

Henry took in the picture of his naked wife and his worst enemy, and a look of pure fury crossed his face unlike anything Margaret had ever seen. She recoiled in fear, realizing how disgraceful she must look.

The duke smirked and said in a victorious tone, "Welcome, Viscount Rolantry. I am glad that you could make it. I told you that it would be worth your time if you came."

Clenching his fists at his side, Henry said, "I can see that. I suppose this was meant to enlighten me as to the 'true nature' of my wife."

Richard's eyes gleamed with smug triumph. He was quite

aware of the power of his untucked shirt, undone pants, and disheveled hair. "Perhaps, but more importantly, I want you to realize that all this time you thought she has been making love to you, she really has been thinking of me."

"Thank you for your invitation, *Your Grace*. It has given me a great deal of insight to the character of the woman I have loved all my life," he said as he stonily stared at his wife. "I believe I was quite mistaken about her."

Margaret darted away from Richard and quickly grabbed the remnants of her dress, pulling it against her naked body as she clamored to her husband's side.

Grabbing at the front of Henry's shirt with her free hand, she appealed, "It is not as it appears. He forced me, Henry! I came here to defend you and he forced me!"

Without looking at her, he pushed her away. "I do not want to hear your empty excuses. I expect your things to be packed and you to have yourself removed to the London estate by tomorrow's eve." He looked down at her without revealing anything. "I never want to see you again."

She latched on to him, holding on for dear life, and begged as she tried to look him in the eyes. "Please, Henry, you must not send me away! Please, you cannot let him do this to us. This is what he wants. He wants to separate us."

"*You* are the one who has separated us. You wanted your freedom. Now you will have it!"

He tried to push her away again, but she held on even tighter. "No, Henry, do not push me away." She pleaded with her eyes. "I love you."

She saw a quick look of anguish and then nothing. He yanked free of her grasp and moved past her, putting his back to her.

"As for you, Duke of Witherton, I plan to see you on the dueling field tomorrow. I challenge you to a duel over the...," he paused for a moment, and then growled out, "*honor of my wife.*" With that, he turned around and headed for the door.

Margaret reached out for Henry again, but Richard came up beside her, pulled her arm down to her side, and put his arm around her.

She tried to pull away, but he would not let her. "How grand, a duel. Will it be swords or pistols?" he said to Henry with amazing levity.

Henry turned back around to face him and blanched at the sight of him holding his wife.

"Swords, and make sure to bring your second. I want it to be known that it was fair." His eyes flickered to his wife and then back to Richard. "I will leave you two to finish what I have interrupted."

Henry opened one of the doors and slipped out. And it was in that moment, as Margaret heard the closing of the door, not only to her life with Henry but also to any chance of happiness, that she realized how much she truly loved her husband.

Margaret turned on Richard. "How dare you let me take the fall for your disgusting act! You monstrous fiend! I cannot believe that I ever thought I loved you!"

He gave her a sinister smile. "My dear, this really is your

entire fault. I offered you an honorable way out. You could have married me, but you chose to marry him instead. I tried to convince you to be with me, I even planned your abduction, framed Baron Wollingleer for it, and then paid him to leave town quietly to make sure no one found out. I had hoped to rescue you and win you back, but your idiot of a husband beat me to it."

As she looked at him, Margaret realized the horrifying truth. Voicing her suspicions, she yelled, "This was all planned. This whole night was staged to destroy my husband." Then another realization struck her as she added in a defeated tone, "You never *loved* me. You only used me to get at Henry. Every dance, every word, every kiss was part of your plot to ruin Henry." She slumped forward and shook her head in self-disgust. "And I fell for it."

"You saw what you wanted to see, and I did genuinely find you attractive. I even grew to have feelings for you, but yes, it was all part of my plan to destroy the Viscount Rolantry. Of course, I cannot offer you marriage now. I mean, not after you have been disgraced. But I will take you as my mistress." He smirked with pride. "I can offer you far more as my mistress than your husband ever could as his wife." He leaned forward and whispered, "And I promise that I will please you far more than he ever did."

She leaned back in loathing and slapped him with all her might. The crack resounded through the room. "I will never be your mistress!"

He raised his hand to slap her back but restrained

himself. "How dare you hit me! I will have you, Margaret. This I vow."

Shoving him away, she screamed, "If I ever see you again, I *will* kill you!" She pushed past him and fled his estate, crying with tears that had not been shed since her brother's death.

CHAPTER 22

They met at the break of dawn—the common backdrop for such an occasion as a duel.

Henry, being the novice that he was when it came to duels, had his work cut out for him since Witherton, being the rake and cad that he was, had been in his fair share of "calling outs." Many a woman's reputations had found their undoing at the hands of the duke, and many husbands and fathers had found themselves at the end of the duke's sword because of it.

Margaret, of course, was not allowed to attend since duels were strictly a gentlemen's affair. No commoners or women would be allowed.

And so she waited anxiously to find out what was to happen to the two most important men in her life. One man she loved, while the other she despised with all her being.

But nothing prepared her for the account the Earl of Bunsdure had the unsavory duty to deliver.

Both arrived dressed in their best suits, boots shined, carrying their finest swords. There were no greetings, and no introductions were necessary. The only indication of any acknowledgment between the two was a slight nod from Henry to Witherton and a sardonic smirk returned from the duke.

Then the two noblemen took their five paces, turned, bowed, and drew their swords.

Witherton pounced first. It seemed that his resentfulness aided him well, keeping him alert and on the offense.

Henry, no doubt, was fueled by his anger and was battling to keep any issues besides the duel from entering his mind.

Every time Henry managed to get a thrust or slash in, Witherton matched it with two of his own, then followed with a fresh attack.

It was visible to everyone present, including the duke, that Henry had lost his edge since leaving the military. Once a superb swordsman, after leaving Her Majesty's royal ranks, he had no need to keep up training.

Witherton, however, had been plotting, planning, and hoping that one day it would come to this. It was quite clear the duke had spent countless hours preparing for the destruction of his enemy.

But from out of nowhere, after seeming like he had nothing left in him, Henry slashed out fiercely and grazed the duke's upper right arm.

Pushed by his embarrassment that a mere viscount had drawn the first blood, the duke lunged forward ferociously.

Henry, now sweating profusely, managed to dodge the attack. However, he did not have time to see the second swing coming.

The sword dug deeply into Henry's chest, pushing between his ribs and piercing his heart.

He fell to the ground, and it only took moments before the blackness claimed him.

The duke's winning blow destroyed Margaret's every chance of happiness.

~

Catherine had carried out Henry's wishes and made sure that Margaret's banishment to the London estate was fulfilled.

"Leave, Margaret. Just the very sight of you makes me sick." Catherine turned away from her sister-in-law. "I believed in you. I trusted you to be faithful to my brother. But the whole time you were plotting with his worst enemy to bring about his destruction." She turned back around and seethed, "Now Henry is dead, and it is because of you!"

Margaret did not even have the will to fight the lies any longer. She said nothing to contradict what Catherine thought. No one would believe her anyway.

Henry made sure the scandal was covered up so there

would be no taint to the Rolantry name. But, possibly because he doubted her all along, he had changed the will from Margaret being his sole heir to Catherine. The only stipulation was if he had had a child, that the child would inherit everything. But he had died with no children and believing his wife was unfaithful.

She had not even been allowed to attend his funeral as Catherine had secretly kept her from it, telling everyone that Margaret was too grief-stricken to attend.

Margaret was a shell of her former self. Nothing mattered to her anymore. The degradation and humiliation of that night would stay with her forever. It took days for her to even be able to look at herself in the mirror. Just the sight of her body and the now fading bruises made her feel dirty, tainted. She had no idea how to get past the ugliness of those horrible moments.

The pain the memories caused was beyond description, and what made it worse was that Henry had died believing that she had let it happen willingly, that she had betrayed him.

She knew it would be easy to blame God for what happened. To be honest, a few months back, she would have. But the hardest part of all was admitting that she needed to place the blame where it belonged, and at least in part, it was her own fault. She had let the duke in and let him trick her into falling for his lies and manipulation.

Catherine had a right to be angry with her. If she had

listened to her father when he had told her his suspicions of the duke and never fought her marriage to Henry, Henry never would have had a reason to doubt her loyalty. Instead, she had let her infatuation with the duke cloud her judgment, and she had played right into his hands.

CHAPTER 23

*H*er faith in God was the only thing that got her through the initial weeks after the death of Henry. Margaret had wanted to die with him, and part of her felt like she had. Her eyes were swollen from countless tears, her face was drawn from lack of sleep, and she only ate when Sarah forced her.

Most of the time, she could not find the will to do anything. She would lie in her bed and pray for God to give her strength to survive the loss of her husband.

Two months after her husband's death, while Margaret was staying at the London estate, God gave her hope when she discovered that she was with child, the heir to the title and wealth of the Rolantry name.

"My lady, it is the only thing that explains why your monthly visit has not come for two months and why you have been getting sick in the morning. Those are the symptoms of it, and I have suspected it for weeks now," Sarah said with a strained smile.

"With child? With child! I cannot be with child. That would be too unfair."

But even though she hated that Henry would never know the child they had created together, Margaret found comfort that God had given her a piece of Henry that she could hold on to even though he was gone.

Margaret still could not believe it to be true, but in the end, she knew it would be the only thing to keep Catherine from ruining her and turning her out. God had saved her life and reputation by giving her Henry's son. She would honor that gift by choosing to be a good mother. God and her child were the only two things she had left to live for, and she was not going to let either of them down.

"So, I have been told that you are with child."

Margaret was taken aback by the coldness in the voice of the girl she considered a sister. She had hoped as time passed that Catherine's anger towards her would have dissipated, but it was just the opposite. It seemed as if the girl hated the very sight of her.

"It is true. God has chosen to give me a piece of Henry in the form of a child."

"*If* it is Henry's heir," Catherine said with firm doubt as she looked at Margaret, who was sitting at the windowsill.

Margaret flinched at the hurtful comment. She had refused to even contemplate the idea that it could be otherwise. Quickly, she defended the unborn baby. "This *is* Henry's son, and the future Viscount Rolantry."

It had to be. Just by sheer odds the baby had to be Henry's child. They had been together for more times than the one night that the duke had forced himself on her. She believed in her heart that it was her late husband's final gift to her.

"Well, we shall see quite quickly if the baby is *not* what you claim it to be. If the child is Henry's, I will be taking it and raising it as the Rolantry heir *without* your help."

"You cannot take my child!"

"I can and I will. If you try to fight me, I will reveal *everything* surrounding Henry's death and ruin you. Then both you and your child will have nothing. If you want this baby to have a future, you *will* relinquish your claim to it."

"You do not know the truth about what happened, Catherine. Despite what you have been told, I was deceived and attacked by the Duke of Witherton. He planned for Henry to find us after he forced me. I *never* betrayed your brother! I loved him more than anything in this world. I still do."

Margaret forced the tears back, not wanting to cry since she knew it was not good for the baby, and her crying would only make Catherine think she was trying to manipulate her.

"You can save your breath, Margaret. Henry told me everything before he died. I suspected at some point that you would try to persuade me with your lies. I *believed* in you, trusted you, and you betrayed not only me but also the most important person in my life. And that betrayal cost him his life. I will never forgive you for it. Never!"

Standing up, she reached out, wanting to make Catherine understand, but Catherine stepped back, visibly disgusted with Margaret and not wanting to even be touched by her.

"Once the baby is born, I will come back and make the decision of what will be done with it. You better hope and pray that it is Henry's child, because if it is not, you will have to figure out how to survive on your own. Additionally, there is the possibility that the duke will want to lay claim to his bastard."

Margaret sucked in a deep breath and held it tightly. Panic began to consume her and, suddenly, the room started to spin. She gripped the edge of the windowsill to balance herself. What was she going to do?

She suspected an additional reason Catherine was determined to acquire her baby as Henry's heir was because it would secure Catherine's future as the head of the Rolantry family. The only way Catherine would remain in control of the Rolantry fortune would be through an heir. She needed Margaret's child in order to hold on to her brother's title and wealth.

Catherine was going to take her son if he was Henry's, and if the baby did not look like Henry, they would be left at the mercy of Witherton. Both outcomes made her tremble with fear, and she knew she had to figure out a way to keep Catherine from trying to destroy her.

Desperately trying to think of a way of making Catherine give up her claim to the baby, she realized she had one bit of truth that could make Catherine back down. Margaret said as delicately as she could, "Catherine, you have forgotten one thing. I *know* the truth about you. I was the one who came up with the idea of turning you into a legitimate sister to Henry and heir to the Rolantry title. If you try to take my child, I will be forced to tell everyone the truth. You would lose everything and possibly even spend the rest of your life in prison for perpetrating a fraud on the nobility. Is taking away my son really worth losing everything you have?"

Catherine glared at Margaret for several long seconds before replying in a spiteful tone, "First, I owe it to my brother to make sure that *his* son is not raised by the likes of *you*. Secondly, who do you think everyone will believe? A bitterly disgraced harlot who caused her own husband's death or a grieving sister who has an unblemished reputation? You can make all the allegations you want, but given your known history with the duke and the circumstances around Henry's death, no one will believe you."

Margaret hated to admit it, but Catherine was right. Even though she knew the truth, she could not use it to help herself if no one believed her because of her scandalous past.

"Take good care of my nephew and enjoy him while you have the chance. I suggest you use this time to prepare yourself to hand him over to me once he is born. You may have taken my brother from me, but you will not succeed in keeping his baby."

With those final ominous words, Catherine turned around and walked out of the London estate.

~

Margaret found herself sitting at the windowsill again. It was the only thing that brought her comfort. She would stare out, searching for something—anything that would ease the pain. She wanted to feel whole again, not broken off into pieces. But all she saw when she looked out the window were dirty streets filled with faceless people who looked just as miserable as she felt.

The first few months of her pregnancy were filled with so much emotional pain that Margaret had not been sure if she could survive without Henry. But she knew she could not allow herself to fall into deep despair, although at every moment it threatened to overwhelm her. She had to remain alive for her child's sake. She owed it to Henry.

It was hard coming to terms with the fact that all her plans for a future with Henry were never going to come true. Her girlish dreams of growing old with him and raising horses and babies on their country estate would never come to pass. She was left clutching at memories that were already beginning to fade.

And what was worse, what tore her up the most, was that she had never told him that she loved him until it was too late. She had denied it over and over again, and now she realized that she had probably loved him from the beginning. She was just too afraid to admit it.

Now he was gone and she could never tell him that she loved him more than anything. She would never be able to tell him that, in the few short months that they were married, he had made her happier than she had ever been in her whole life.

Daily, she was haunted by the fact that he died hating her, thinking that she had betrayed him. And every day, she had to live knowing that she had allowed Richard to use her to destroy her own husband.

But when the bitterness threatened to take hold and overwhelm her, Margaret would remind herself that she had their baby growing inside her. She needed to give all that love she had for Henry to their son. And she knew it was a boy. Somehow, she just did. He was Henry's son, and he would be her constant reminder of the love she had with her husband.

Looking out the window, Margaret rubbed her stomach and felt her son kick. He was growing stronger every day. She was at the end of her eighth month and the time for him to come into the world was fast approaching.

Smiling at the thought of holding him soon, she cherished her child. If it had not been for him, she knew that she would not have survived the loss of Henry. It was the knowledge that their child depended on her to live that made her get up every day and fight to survive. If she gave up, then she would forfeit his life as well.

She remembered how she forced herself to leave the window and take care of herself. It had taken such an effort just to eat, to sleep—just to do the minimum to get by. But she continued to push forward and, slowly but surely, it got easier.

It was still difficult, and often she had to remind herself that she still had something to live for: her son. She also cherished the little reminders of her husband: grooming her horse, taking a bath, even eating breakfast. He was like a ghost that haunted her and never allowed her peace. But at the same time, she wanted him to haunt her. Margaret wanted that connection with her husband. She needed it.

Even though the days were unavoidably hard, the nights were even worse. Sometimes, when she was able to sleep, she would dream that Henry was still alive and that they were still together. In her dreams, she could still feel his touch and feel his love. All the pain and anger that had been between them in the end was not there, only joy and desire.

Then she would wake up, swearing she smelt his scent, and would reach over to touch him but would find emptiness beside her. She would curl up in a ball and wait for morning to come. And when it came, she still had to drag herself out of bed and shake off the depression that crept up on her during those sleepless nights.

Other nights, her pleasant dreams were replaced by

nightmares filled with the horror of *that* night. She would feel it all over again, Richard ripping her apart emotionally and forcing his way into her body.

Then she would see Henry's face, filled with disgust and contempt. She would feel the humiliation, the hurt, and degradation all over again, and she would wake up in a thick sweat, panting with terror-filled tears.

But even though she feared she had been broken for the rest of her life, she managed to keep her mind intact through prayer and reading the Word of God. It helped her to meditate on the Psalms and how David, the anointed king of God, survived tremendous loss. The Lord had seen him through assassination attempts, living without a home for years, and the death of a child. God could and would show her how to live without Henry.

CHAPTER 24

*S*itting at the window like so many times before, Margaret was overtaken by an unbearable amount of pain racking her body. She had been told what birth pains were supposed to feel like, but something was horribly wrong.

Quickly, she realized it was far too early for her to be giving birth. What would happen if she had the baby this early? Would he be able to survive? And if she did not make it through the process, who would take her child?

Margaret stood and started to walk towards the door in order to get help but stopped midway. Leaning against the wall, she doubled over as fits of pain hit her.

Forcing herself to breathe and make the air return to her lungs, she screamed with a shrill voice, "Sarah, I need you! Something is wrong with the baby!"

Trying to combat the fear, Margaret prayed, *Lord, protect*

my unborn son and keep us safe. You gave him to me for a purpose, and I know you will not take him away from me now. I put our lives in your hands and believe that, in faith, you will see us through this!

She heard commotion down the hall and scurrying feet. Then the doors burst open and Sarah rushed to her side, followed by several other servants.

"What is it, my lady? What is happening?"

"I do not know, but I cannot even move. The pain is unbearable!"

She screamed as another wave of agony descended on her.

"I need you to send someone to get the doctor," Margaret said in a breathless voice as Sarah started to give orders.

"But it is too early to have the baby, my lady."

"I know, but my son's strong. We will get through this."

She grabbed the edge of Sarah's sleeve as her companion led her over to the couch. "Listen to me. We need...." She stopped talking as she sucked in and gasped as another wave hit her. "We need... to go with the plan... we discussed. Get the unknown... doctor that I privately... contacted. Catherine cannot... be informed of the... birth." Worry clouded Sarah's eyes as Margaret added, "You know what will happen if she finds out."

Margaret watched through groggy eyes as the doctor left her

room. Sarah was sitting next to her as she tried to listen to the conversation between her other servants and the doctor outside her room.

Motty asked, "How is Lady Margaret and the baby?"

"She is having severe complications, and it is not clear whether either of them will make it through the night."

Francisca asked, "Can we see them?"

"It would be best if they rest right now. They are both weak and need to sleep if they are going to get better."

Patting Margaret's hand, Sarah said, "I will be right back, my lady. I need to take care of everything with the doctor."

Sarah went out of the room and Margaret heard her say to the doctor, "Remember, you say nothing to no one about the countess giving birth tonight. Here is the promised money."

A few minutes later, Margaret heard the outer door to the street shut.

Motty asked Sarah tentatively, "The doctor did not really answer us. How is Lady Margaret?"

The distress in Sarah's voice was unmistakable, as she replied, "Not well."

Both girls gasped in worry.

"But I will do whatever it takes to make sure that she does get better, and I am sure all of you will as well. I need to go back in and sit with her."

Francisca asked quietly, "Can I sit with her too?"

There was a pause before Sarah replied, "Yes, I think it

would be good for her to have a couple of us nearby, but you must be quiet as she needs her rest."

Sarah entered the room, followed by Francisca and Motty.

~

"What is going on? Where am I?"

Her hands automatically went to rub her stomach and she realized that her child was no longer there.

"Where is my son?" she asked, groggily.

Sarah's eyebrows shot up in surprise. "You gave birth two days ago but fell unconscious right afterward. How do you know that you had a boy?"

"I have always known that I was carrying a boy," she said matter-of-factly. "Where is he?"

"He is with his wet nurse currently."

Margaret blinked several times and focused her thoughts. She needed to see her son. "I want to see him. Bring him to me."

Sarah stood. "Yes, my lady, I will go get him right away."

She stopped Sarah with her voice. "What of Catherine? Has she found out yet?"

Turning back around, Sarah replied, "No, my lady. Since you gave birth before the expected time, she is currently unaware. I did exactly as you asked and the doctor gave his word that he would tell no one. As for the servants, they are faithful to you and you alone. They will not tell anyone either."

"Good, now bring me my son."

A few minutes passed and Sarah reappeared with a tiny baby in her arms. Gently, she handed him over to his mother. He was the most beautiful thing she had ever seen, perfect in every way, and God had protected both of them during his birth.

Margaret smiled and said, "He has his father's face."

"He is so darling."

"Yes, that he is."

Looking up, she said with a slight nervousness in her voice, "I need you to finish preparing the details for leaving." Margaret directed Sarah to walk over to one of her chests and pull out a billfold of money. "My father hid that away in case we needed it. Take it and secure our passage. Have a bare minimum of my things packed and ready to go, as well as the baby's belongings. We have to be ready to leave in a moment's notice."

"How is the baby fairing, my lady?"

Margaret smiled down at her son. "He is doing exceptionally well."

Sarah walked up and peered over at the one-week-old child. "Have you decided on a name yet?"

"I am going to name him after his father, Henry." She looked up. "Fitting, do you not think?"

"Yes, it is very good idea, my lady."

"Have you heard any news about Catherine?"

Her companion shook her head in denial.

"Good. Remember to have everything ready nevertheless. We have waited to leave far longer than I had originally planned."

"Yes, my lady, your recovery has taken much longer than anyone had anticipated."

The doctor had told Margaret that after she had given birth, she had almost died. Margaret had been concerned while she prepared for her son's birth that her delivery might meet with complications. She knew that her mother had died giving birth to her and her brother due to severe blood loss, and she had known it was possible she might have the same outcome. Luckily, Margaret's doctor had faced similar situations several times with previous deliveries and was able to get the bleeding under control. But due to the excessive amount of blood she had lost, it took Margaret a solid week to finally be back on her feet.

"I realize that, but it is becoming far too risky for us to stay here. Catherine could find out at any moment, and I want to be gone before that happens."

"Of course, my lady. Everything is ready, and we can leave as quickly as needed. I will be back shortly, but I need to go take care of a few final details for our departure."

Sarah left the door ajar and Margaret could hear Francisca say in a frightened tone, "Miss, we have a problem. One of the servants has reported to Catherine about Lady Margaret's delivery. We just found out and she should be here by nightfall."

"How did you find out about this?"

"We found out only by accident. Phillip has always had a big mouth, and he was bragging about how he was going to be rich soon. Then we heard from a servant from one of the outlying estates that Catherine had stopped there last night to rest before continuing on to come here today." She took a breath, then asked, "What are we going to do, miss?"

"The rest of you are going to do nothing. Albert and I are going to take Lady Margaret and the baby and leave. We are not going to say where we are going so that no one knows when Catherine arrives. Prepare a carriage. I must tell our mistress what has happened."

Francisca asked, "Miss, Motty and I have nothing to keep us here. Can we please come with you? We'll help take care of the baby, and I promise we will not get in the way."

Margaret could hear the distress in the girl's voice. Sarah probed, "Why do you ask?"

Francisca replied, "Our loyalty has always been to Lady Margaret. In addition, we have heard that Catherine has started to become cruel with her servants after the loss of her brother. She would surely be harsh to us for being loyal to our mistress."

"I see. In that case, you are both welcome to come along,

but Lady Margaret will not be able to pay you what you currently receive and it will *not* be easy."

Sarah opened the door and stepped through. Margaret glanced up and inquired, "Sarah, I heard everything"

"My lady, we need to be leaving immediately."

Margaret started to stand with the infant in her arms while asking, "I cannot believe it was Phillip." She paused for a moment, realizing that one of her father's servants had betrayed her. "I did not expect that. Phillip was one of my father's most trusted servants. I grew up in the stables he took care of and never would have thought he could do something like this to me."

Pushing her dismay aside, Margaret said, "I cannot dwell on that now. Prepare everything for our departure, and then bring Phillip to me before we leave. Do not let him know we know or he will most likely try to flee before I can confront him."

As Margaret got dressed, she thought about what was happening. She had never believed that she would end up leaving her beloved England. But then, she never would have imagined that she would be a widow at seventeen. So much had changed in the last year, and it was going to change even more now.

First wrapping her son in a thick blanket, she then tucked him back into her arms. Restless, he began to fuss, and she softly hummed him a lullaby. A few moments passed until he settled down and cooed with contentment.

Margaret loved her son, and she was going to do whatever it took to protect him from Catherine's wrath, even if that meant leaving England forever. Gently, she pulled the blanket snuggly around her sleeping son and quietly left the room. She made her way down the corridor and came into the reception hall of her London home.

She stopped a few feet away from her once-loyal servant who was standing between two of Margaret's other servants who were holding him by his arms. Phillip pulled free from their grasp and gave an indifferent look towards Margaret.

Trying to mask the hurt in her voice but not succeeding, she accused, "Why did you tell Lady Catherine about my baby's birth?"

Greedily, he said, "She offered me more money than you have. You have nothing left to offer any of us. Everyone knows your father's estate was destitute and the viscount left Lady Catherine everything in his will. I knew where my future had hope. She is going to reward me greatly for my help."

"I pity you if you really think she values your 'help.' You are only a pawn that she used to get at me." She shook her head in pity.

He scoffed, "You say what you want, but I *will* get my money, and that is all that matters."

"I trusted you, Phillip. You have known me since I was a little girl, and I have always been good to you. I do not understand how you could do this to me."

Angrily, he spit out, "You did this to yourself when you decided to make a cuckold of the viscount! I owe no loyalty to a woman who doesn't even honor her own marriage vows."

Shocked that he would be so hateful, she replied, "You do not know what you are talking about. I thought you were above listening to gossip."

"It is not gossip if it is the truth."

Realizing that no matter what she said he was determined to believe the worst of her, Margaret turned away and said over her shoulder, "Take him away."

For the first time, Margaret recognized that leaving England would be the only way to not only escape Catherine but the scandal that threatened to be exposed at a moment's notice. Too many people knew about her sordid past with the duke and her late husband. Every moment she remained in England, there was a chance her reputation would be ruined, and then there would be no hope for either her or her son.

Margaret looked at Sarah and asked, "Are we ready to leave, Sarah? Do you have everything we need?"

Sarah nodded.

"Then let us be on our way. It is finally time to go to France and find out what happened to my brother."

And with that, Margaret made the choice to leave her life in England behind forever.

PREVIEW OF THE FRENCH ENCOUNTER (BOOK 2)

1863 Le Havre, France

*L*ady Margaret, Countess of Renwick and widow of Henry William Wiltshire, the Viscount Rolantry, held on to the rail of the steamboat. As she approached the French shoreline, her long, raven locks blew in the wind and she could feel the fall air on her pale skin.

As she clutched the vessel's edge, she wondered what lay ahead for her. Not only was she afraid, since it was her first time on the open sea, but also because everything was so unknown. She had barely been out of her province in England, and now she was about to step foot in a foreign country. This new place held the possibility of a completely fresh future for her and her newborn son.

She never thought she would leave her homeland of England, let alone run away in the middle of the night because she feared for the safety of her family. But with her parents dead and having no family to protect her, she had no other recourse.

The events that led to her fleeing to France still haunted her. She would never forget the brutal attack on her body by Richard Charles Crawley III, the Duke of Witherton, or how he set the whole ordeal in motion to look like she willingly betrayed her husband. The horrified look of anguish on Henry's face when he saw what seemed to be an unfaithful liaison would not leave her. She had tried to convince him it was not her doing and that she had been trying to protect him because she loved him, but he did not believe her when she told him that the duke had tricked her so he could use her to hurt Henry.

So much mistrust and damage had been done by her naïve belief that she had been in love with the duke that, by the time she uttered the words out loud, saying "I love you" could not fix what had been destroyed. Her husband died in a duel over her honor, believing she never loved him. Margaret could not reconcile her guilt from his death.

As punishment, her late husband's sister, Catherine, enforced the banishment Henry had placed on her, confining her to their London estate. In an ironic twist, two months into her exile, she found out that she was with child. It was only her faith in God and her choice to live for her unborn son that made it possible for Margaret to survive.

Every day had been a battle to live without the love of her life. Basic things like eating and sleeping felt like impossible feats. And the most difficult part was living in fear of the outcome of the paternity of her son. She recalled Catherine saying to her, *"Once the baby is born, I will come back and make the decision of what will be done with it. You better hope and pray that it is Henry's child, because if it is not, you will have to figure out how to survive on your own. Additionally, there is the possibility that the duke will want to lay claim to his bastard."*

But God protected her. Through her exile, she was given the opportunity to plan her escape. When she gave birth to her son, whom she named Henry after her late husband, she was able to keep Catherine from intercepting her and carrying out her plans.

Even though she had never been to France, Margaret knew more about it than any other country. Her twin brother, Randall, had been lost at sea when his ship went down outside of France. She had vigorously researched everything there was to know about the country, hoping that one day she might be able to take a trip to France to find him. But her father dealt with Randall's presumed death by focusing on anything other than finding out what happened to him, which left no room to allow her to pursue her hopes of finding her brother alive.

Flash forward eight years and Margaret had finally made it to France in the most unexpected way. When she decided to flee the country, she made the decision to go there so she could carry out her long-hidden plan to search for her brother. If she had to leave behind everything she loved and knew, it was not going to be in vain. If her brother was alive, she was going to find him.

As Margaret stepped off the ship, she was greeted by a tall, well-dressed gentleman with a thick French accent. "Welcome to France, Countess. I am so delighted to see you again. I am glad that you have arrived safe, and I have arranged for you to stay at my estate."

Pierre Girard, the Vidame of Demoulin, was an old family friend and had visited her family right before her marriage to Henry. He had approached her father to discuss the possibility of courting her, but her father had declined his offer, opting to keep his promise to Henry's late father instead.

Margaret studied the vidame; he had a chiseled body that was made evident by his tailored, stately suit in light grey. He was quite handsome with his straight, jet-black hair that stood out in contrast against his pale skin. His face was set off by his dark brown eyes that drew her in and held her attention. He was confident but not arrogant, which was refreshing in a nobleman, and there was something about him that exuded sensuality.

She had not been able to see Pierre's admirable qualities when he previously visited because she had been infatuated with the Duke of Witherton. Nothing else mattered to her, and she had no idea who the duke really was or of what he was capable.

When Margaret realized she was in danger from two different directions, she knew she had to leave England to protect her son. She discreetly contacted the vidame, via letter, to ask if he would be willing to allow her to stay with him while she made more permanent arrangements. She explained her travel and stay with him should be kept quiet as there were safety concerns for her family if they remained in England. The vidame had agreed to her request, and Margaret was relieved to find somewhere safe to stay while she figured out what to do next.

"Countess, by title I am a protector of land and people alike. I assure you that you will be safe and I will not allow any harm to come to you or your son while you are under my care." The young man bowed deeply, and as he came up, he took Margaret's hand and kissed the top of it.

She smiled softly at him and spoke in flawless French, "Thank you for your hospitality, my lord."

His mouth formed an appreciative grin. "You speak French beautifully, Countess. Tell me, how is it that you came to speak my language so fluently?"

"I had a deep... interest in your country since I was a young child and wanted to know every detail about it, including how to speak the language. At my insistence, my father hired a French tutor."

He took her hand and put it in the crook of his arm. "Come, I will escort you to my estate, and then we can discuss what your plans shall be while you stay with me."

"I am honored that you have done as much as you already have for us. I am truly grateful."

"After our last encounter in England, you should know by now that I would do anything you ask of me."

She blushed at the compliment. It seemed Pierre's interest in her had not dissipated since the last time they were together. "Your generosity is just one of your numerous admirable qualities, my lord."

Hearing a noise behind her, they both looked at her entourage. With a hint of mirth, Pierre commented, "It does not seem you travel light, Countess."

Margaret looked at her devoted servants, Albert, Sarah, Motty, and Francisca, who chose to follow her to France. Along with her son and several pieces of luggage, she could see that she appeared to be ostentatious. However, what the vidame did not know was that this trip had no return date. There was no going home for any of them.

As they walked towards the nearby carriage, Margaret weighed her options on whether to tell the vidame the full details of her predicament. She worried that, if she told him the entire circumstances surrounding her sordid past, he would look at her differently. She did not think she could handle another person judging her for something that was out of her control. She needed the vidame to remain on her side, so she chose to keep the intimate details surrounding her reasons for coming to France private.

"I hope that France meets and exceeds all of your expectations," the vidame said as he helped Margaret up into the carriage.

She turned her head and looked down at him with her deep violet eyes, replying, "I am sure that it will, my lord."

~

The vidame's estate was expansive, one of the biggest in which she had ever been, and she thoroughly valued all the comforts. It had been a long time since she had been treated so well. When Henry died, Catherine had left her with a skeleton staff and a small stipend for her needs. She had saved almost all of it, along with the hidden money she had from her father's safety deposit box, for her plan to flee England. She had spent the entirety of her pregnancy living like a pauper.

"So, how are you settling into Parintene? Do you approve of my home?"

Margaret took a sip of her wine and then replied, "Yes, Pierre, it is lovely."

The two of them had grown acquainted over the two weeks she had stayed at his home and started calling each other by their given names.

"I believe that we are friends again, like we were as children. Do you agree?"

Smiling, she nodded. "We are fast becoming that, I agree. I cannot thank you enough for taking us in like this. I have not felt this secure in almost a year's time."

"I am pleased you feel safe. I also hope you are enjoying the amenities."

"Most assuredly. Your home provides a myriad of activities. As you may have guessed, the stable is my preferred destination."

"I ascertained as much from my previous visit to your home. I remember you wearing that lovely riding habit and knew you would be partial. I am glad the stables are to your liking. I had them refurbished for your arrival, as well as purchased additional horses for your use."

Margaret was impressed by Pierre going to such a prodigious extent to make her stay agreeable. She found it soothing being in the stables, as she had always found comfort in riding horses.

"I appreciate your care in providing such lavish accommodations. Your stables are magnificent and the horses are wonderful. However, I miss my own horse, Charlie, terribly."

Charlotte's Pride—or Charlie, as Margaret called her—was the Arabian filly her family had been working towards preparing for show in England before everything went awry in her life. Margaret had spent countless hours in the stables making sure the trainers did everything right. As a woman, she was unable to do the work herself, but she had read comprehensively on the subject and participated as much as possible. Her father had allowed her to make most decisions in regard to their estate horses, and her late husband had given her the same latitude with the ones they owned. But when she had fled, she was unable to take most of her possessions with her, and a horse was out of the question. Giving up so much, Margaret wanted one day to be able to reclaim part of her hopes and dreams by producing her own line of purebred horses. She yearned to find the finances and land to do it, but all of that would have to wait until she found her brother, if in fact he was still alive. If she did, they could move away together, somewhere remote where no one would ever find them.

"I am sorry you were unable to bring her with you. I know how much you cared for her."

Margaret looked away and tried to hide her sadness at the thought of never seeing Charlie again. "Thank you. It has been difficult coping with the many losses."

Pierre had proven a faithful and devoted confidant, and she knew that keeping her past from him would not serve either of them well. He could not help protect her if he did not know from whom he was doing the protecting, so Margaret had explained her entire situation to him—at least, the broad strokes of it. She still could not bear to discuss the details with anyone. The pain and humiliation felt as fresh as it did the night the duke forced himself on her.

"I am glad that your father was friends with mine. If not, my son might be in the clutches of someone else by now."

He frowned. "You are sure that you do not want me to help you with your situation? I know many influential people who could take care of your *problem* for you. You would not have to worry any longer."

She shook her head. "This particular situation is something that will not just go away simply by contacting the right person."

Margaret watched as Pierre smirked and raised an eyebrow, as if amused. He then stated, with a hint of danger in his voice, "I would argue it depends upon the person you contact. There are many types of people in this world, and I know the right types that could make both of your problems disappear."

She realized immediately that he meant he could make the duke and Catherine "disappear." Though tempting, she could not be responsible for the death of another human being, even one as vile as Witherton or as hateful as Catherine. Her new relationship with God made her value all human life, and she truly believed in the idea that anyone could be saved. It was hard to accept that meant even the duke, but at the core of her beliefs, she truly believed everyone was salvageable. It was not her business to save them, but it also was not her place to remove the chance of redemption. She left justice for the Lord to exact one day and preferred to focus on her future.

Uncomfortable with the conversation, Margaret changed the topic. "There *is* something else with which you can help me. I am in need of hiring an investigator. Could you help me locate one?"

Pierre leaned back in consideration for a few moments before replying, "I have used one on occasion myself. The one I employ is exceptional, as well as quite discreet. I can set up an appointment with him whenever you wish. But I ask you, why is it that you need to hire one, Margaret?"

As she stared at the wineglass, she absentmindedly

tapped the stem with her fingertips. After a few moments, she looked over at Pierre. "I need to find my brother."

He furrowed his brows together in confusion. "I do not understand what you mean. I was under the impression that you had no family left. I had been informed of your father's death, and I went to school with your brother Randall before he was killed."

"No, Pierre, I know Randall never died in that shipwreck. If he had, I would have felt it. We have a special bond as twins, and I just know that he is still alive." She glanced over at the window and continued as she stared out. "Randall is one of the main reasons I came to France. I have wanted to search for him for years but have never been able to leave England. You might think that I am on a fool's errand, and you might even be right, but I have to know for certain." She brought her focus back to Pierre. "Since I am here now, I need to try to find him. He is the only family I have left."

Pierre gestured to one of the servants, who immediately came to his side. He whispered something in the servant's ear and then turned his attention back to Margaret.

"I just sent word to Josef Mulchere. He will help you find your brother."

"Thank you again, Pierre."

"I understand your reason for coming here now, but I have to admit I had hoped, before your disclosure, that you chose to come to France because of me. You know I had been interested in pursuing a courtship with you before you married Henry. My feelings for you have not altered."

"You are a dear friend, Pierre, but I am not ready for a romantic relationship. I am still in mourning over Henry's death."

Pierre nodded. "I would expect nothing less, but when you are ready, I will be waiting."

Margaret's smile faded and a pang of sadness took hold in her. "You should not wait for me. I am in no condition to be with anyone. I fear I am broken beyond repair."

"You give entirely too much power to *that* man. The duke did not destroy you. The woman who sits before me is kinder, wiser, and stronger than the one I knew back in England."

"You have always seen the best in me, Pierre, even when we were children. When I see you, I think of happier times, when you and I, along with Randall and Henry, played in the family gardens. Life was so much easier back then. So much loss has occurred since those days."

"You have had more than your fair share of misfortunes. I do, indeed, hope you find your brother. I think it would do the both of us a world of good. When he was lost, it was one of the hardest times in my life, and I know it was for you as well."

"Randall's disappearance left a hole in all our lives."

"Agreed, but there is hope he can be returned to us. If he is alive, Monsieur Mulchere will find him."

The French Encounter available now.

ACKNOWLEDGMENTS

My debut novel has been realized, and it would not be possible without those who supported me. Since I can remember, writing is the only thing I love to do, and my deepest desire is to share my talent with others.

First and foremost, I am eternally grateful to Jesus, my lord and savior, who created me with this "writing bug" DNA.

In addition, many thanks go to:

My husband, Dustin, and three daughters, Katie, Julie, and Nikki, for loving me and supporting me during all my late-night writing marathons and coffee-infused mornings.

My mother, Connie, for being my first and most honest critic, now and always. As a little girl, sleeping under your desk during late-night deadlines for the local paper showed me what being a dedicated writer looked like.

My angels in heaven: my grandmother, who passed away

in 2001; my infant son, Dylan, who was taken by SIDS three years ago; and my father, who left us this past year.

My good friend and fellow indie author Alexia Purdy who answered all my questions about this process and showed me the ropes as well as designed the incredible cover for my book.

Hot Tree Editing and their beta readers for doing such an impeccable job helping me prepare my writing for publication.

To my ARC Angels for taking the time to read my story and give valuable feedback.

To the Jenna Brandt Books Street Team, who have pounded the virtual streets on the internet, helping to spread the words about my books. Your dedication means a great deal.

ABOUT THE AUTHOR

Jenna Brandt graduated with her BA in English from Bethany College. She is an ongoing contributor for The Mighty website, and her blog has been featured on Yahoo Parenting, The Grief Toolbox, ABC News and Good Morning America websites.

Writing is her passion, with her focus in the Christian historical genre. Her books span from the Victorian to Western eras with elements of romance, suspense and faith.

Jenna also enjoys cooking, reading, and spending time with her three young daughters and husband where they live in the Central Valley of California. Jenna is also active in her local church, including serving on the first impressions team and writing features for the church's creative team.

A NOTE FROM THE AUTHOR

I hope you have enjoyed *The English Proposal* and plan to continue on this journey with Margaret throughout the series. Your opinion and support matters, so I would greatly appreciate you taking the time to leave a review. Without dedicated readers, a storyteller is lost. Thank you for investing in Margaret's story.

Jenna Brandt

Made in the USA
Columbia, SC
09 February 2021

32645467R00178